A KALEIDOSCOPE OF
FAIRIES
& FABLES

A KALEIDOSCOPE OF
FAIRIES & FABLES

by Hans Andersen, Aesop, Rudyard Kipling & The Brothers Grimm

re~told by Robert Mathias

HAMLYN

Published in 1988 by
The Hamlyn Publishing Group Limited
a division of Paul Hamlyn Publishing
Michelin House, 81 Fulham Road, London SW3 6RB

ISBN 0 600 55721 9

Printed in Hong Kong by Mandarin Offset

These fairy tales and fables were originally published in *Aesop's Fables*
published in 1983; *The Stories of Hans Andersen* published in 1985; *Tales
from the Brothers Grimm* published in 1986 and *Just So Stories* by Rudyard
Kipling published in 1987. The stories were re-told by Robert Mathias and
were published by The Hamlyn Publishing Group Limited.

CONTENTS

The Little Mermaid

HAVE YOU HEARD, that deep in the sea, live the mer-people? They live where the ocean is the bluest of blues and as deep as twenty mountains, piled one on top of the other.

At the deepest, bluest part is the palace of the mer-king. Its walls are built of crimson and white coral and its roof is tiled with lustrous oyster shells which sparkle as their tiny pearls blink in the filtering sunbeams. Tall windows, laced with the finest fan coral, gleam with the glow of pure amber taken from the belly of a whale. The palace stands in the centre of a great forest of tall trees and thickly clustered bushes, curling and waving in the tilting waters. Fishes, stranger than any you can imagine, slip through the branches and leaves; brightly-coloured flowers open and close as they sift the tide and the painted shells of a thousand creatures line the byways.

The king's dear wife had long since died and now the palace was cared for by his mother. She was kind and thoughtful and was all but a mother to the king's six daughters. They were the fairest princesses in the sea, but the most beautiful was undoubtedly the youngest. Her skin was as soft as the bloom on a rose and her soft eyes were a deep sapphire blue. Of course, like all mermaids, she had no legs, instead, her slender body tapered down into a graceful tail.

Their lives were full of play: they would swim and dart among the trees swirling up the soft silver sand. The sun was their delight and they played in its dappled beams as it filtered through the giant fans, flooding the palace gardens in golden light.

At times the sisters would gather at their grandmother's tail and listen to stories of the land above the water. Their eyes grew wide as she told of ships and men, cities and towns; of creatures called birds that swam through the trees like fishes; of animals with hair and horns that prowled the shoreline and of flowers that filled the air with the sweetest

of perfumes. The youngest mermaid opened her eyes wide.

'Can I see for myself, Grandmama?' she begged, and flipped her tail excitedly. Her grandmother chuckled and drew them close.

'Not yet, my children,' she said softly. 'When you are fifteen, then it will be time. Then you can swim to the top of the sea and watch the ships go by. Close to the shore you'll see cities and trees, but take care when you go that near.'

Must she wait that long thought the youngest. There was a span of five years between her and her eldest sister and she longed for the time to pass quickly; to the day when she would be fifteen.

She was a passive gentle creature and at night she would wait and peer up at the moon. Its great silver bowl would glimmer down into the cool, blue depths and the stars would shiver and twinkle around it. Sometimes a sail would go shadowing by and she wondered what beings kept watch on its decks. Did they know she was there? . . . Waiting.

As year followed year her sisters swam to the shore, and each had returned to tell what they'd seen. One heard the music of church bells chiming; one saw an arrow of wild swans swooping; one saw swimming children and wanted to play, but a dog had appeared and chased her away; the fourth stayed at sea for she had more care, but the dolphins had come and leapt in the air; the fifth sister went where the winter seas ran and sat on an iceberg all through the night, while the ships short-sailed by and their sailors took fright.

The little mermaid was overwhelmed by their stories, but her sisters soon tired of the land and spent their time in the palace gardens, so she heard no more of their tales. At times, though, they would leave her, lonely and sad, and swim off together. They would ride on the tall foaming waves and sing to the seamen on the storm-tossed sailboats. No sailor would dare answer their call, for fear of drowning.

At long last the day of her birthday arrived: she was fifteen! Now, she too, could swim to the land at the top of the sea. Her grandmother gave her a wreath of fine pearls to braid in her hair. She kissed her and took her hand. 'Farewell, my little one,' she said. 'Take care.'

The little mermaid smiled at her grandmother and then at her sisters. 'Farewell,' she said and with a last flip of her tail she rose up through the waters like a sparkling bubble.

Up and up she went until at last the water around her became clear and golden. She was almost at the top of the sea, then, in a blaze of shining, sun-drenched droplets, she burst through the surface.

The rim of the sun was just dropping beneath the nodding waves. The sea was the colour of the darkest rose, streaked with gold and the palest jade. She looked around her and close by saw the tall grey shadow of a three-masted ship. It lifted gently to its anchor on the evening swell and its spidery rigging ran up and down between the tall black masts. High up, one sail remained unfurled and men were dangling their feet from the yard. She heard music drifting over the water and saw more men dancing on the deck. As darkness closed in, lights appeared all over the ship and blinked like coloured stars.

The little mermaid swam closer to the great stern where lamplight flickered over the dark water. She peeped in from the crest of a wave and saw a large, richly-panelled cabin. Inside, she saw many people, finely dressed and laughing, but one among them caught her eye. He was young and handsome with kind dark eyes: he was, indeed, a prince and tonight was his sixteenth birthday. The music and dancing was all part of the celebrations.

After a while he left the cabin and went up on deck, the others following close behind him. She swam round the ship, but suddenly the sky was filled with a million coloured stars. They fell around her and hissed as they hit the water. She was so alarmed she flipped her tail and slipped beneath the surface. After a moment she cautiously popped her head up again.

It was the first time she had seen fireworks and she marvelled at the great display. As each one flared the darkness vanished, but just as soon, as each flame died, the night returned. Her eyes fell once more on the face of the prince, he was so young and handsome.

The night drew on and one by one the lamps went out, but the little mermaid stayed close to the ship hoping to catch just one more glimpse of the prince. Suddenly, as the sea lifted and settled beneath her, she felt a deep rumbling moan come up from the depths of the ocean. Black clouds began to tumble above her: a storm was coming. In an instant the sailors scurried back on deck, scrambled into the rigging and let loose the sails. The anchor chain clanked its way on board and the ship gurgled and hissed as it started to move slowly through the inky waters.

It picked up speed and the little mermaid swam faster to keep up with it. Lightning flashed and thunder echoed through the mountainous black clouds. The waves climbed higher and higher and crashed and pounded against the ship as it ploughed along. One after another the sails were taken in until, in the boiling sea, the ship sailed on with her bare masts flailing the sky like great black bones.

The little mermaid swished and dived through the huge breaking rollers and played in the foaming spindrift; the sailors, however, were white with fear. Suddenly, a giant wave lifted the ship high in the air and as it dropped back, it pitched violently. With a splintering crack the mainmast snapped, swayed and crashed overboard, dragging the stricken ship on to her side. A second great wave rose up and crashed on to the decks, washing the ship from stem to stern and tearing its timbers to pieces. All the lights went out and at last the little mermaid saw the peril that faced the ship and her crew. Fear swept into her heart as spars and timbers slashed through the raging waters and threatened to crush her as she swam alongside. A flash of lightning split the darkness and in its glare she saw the broken ship rolling to its death. The poor wretched seamen were clinging to the tangled ropes that whipped about in the

screaming gale. They were going to drown and she scoured the deck for
sight of the prince. Then, with one last shuddering groan, and a terrible
tearing of timbers, the ship rolled over and slid beneath the boiling sea.

'He must not die,' thought the little mermaid and she dived among
the tangled wreckage that surged and crashed around her. She searched
and searched and just when she was in despair of finding the prince, she
came upon his body. His strength was gone and his eyes were closed; a
moment more and he would have slipped beneath the wind-lashed
waves. She reached out and lifted his head above the foam. The sea
rolled and surged and took them on its course.

When daybreak came the storm had passed. The sun came up and shed an angry orange glow across the still-wild rollers. The prince lay as if asleep in her arms and she gently kissed his brow. Tenderly she kissed him again and hoped with all her heart that he would live.

As the sun climbed higher the waves grew quieter and the little mermaid looked around. In the distance a range of snow-capped mountains loomed greyly over the horizon. She swam towards them and as she got nearer she saw the thickly wooded mountain slopes sweeping down into a green fertile valley. Among a grove of orange trees stood a white-washed building – she was unsure whether it was a church or a house. A small sheltered bay opened up as she swam closer and, gently supporting the prince, she rippled through the clear water and rested his head on the warm silver sand. She was careful to place him well beyond the reach of the tide.

Alone now, she swam away, but she had not gone far when she heard the sound of bells chiming. She turned and saw a group of young girls come out of the white building, which was in fact a church. They laughed and skipped into the garden surrounding it.

She swam swiftly to a rocky islet and watched and waited, not once did she take her eyes off the still figure of the prince.

One of the girls wandered close to the shore and seeing the prince lying on the sand, cried out and ran towards him. Soon, many people had gathered round him and as she watched, he sat up and smiled. He did not look out to sea at all and was unaware that it was the little mermaid who had saved him. She watched them carry him into the church and then, slipping from her hiding place, she dived down into the ocean and swam sadly back to her home.

The little mermaid's sisters asked her again and again what wonders she had seen, but her dreamy head could think only of the prince and of her kisses on his brow and she remained silent.

As day followed day she would swim to the tiny bay where last she'd seen him: the snow on the mountains melted, the trees flowered and bore their fruit, but despite her vigil, she saw no further sign of him.

At last she spoke to her eldest sister and to her surprise she discovered that her sister had not only heard of the prince but had often seen his ship. Once, she said, she had followed it right to the shore where it had anchored beneath a castle. Her sister took her hand and together they swam to the prince's castle. It towered above them on a needle of green rock and from its walls a staircase twisted down to the water's edge.

From then on the little mermaid went frequently to visit the castle. A wide balcony overhung the sea and she would swim beneath it, hoping to catch a glimpse of the prince in his home. She heard the sound of mens' voices and sometimes when he was not there, they would speak of him: how kind and generous he was, how thoughtful and caring for his people and how noble was his spirit. Her admiration for these strange beings increased daily and she wished more and more to become like them and share their land.

There came a day when she was no longer content to watch and wait and she went to her grandmother – she alone could tell her of the land above the sea.

'I know that men drown, Grandmama, but should they not, do they live forever?' she asked. 'Or do they die someday, like us?'

Her grandmother smiled and answered in a soft voice. 'Child, such a question. Yes, my dear, men die – and sooner still than us. We can swim through our lives for a full three hundred years, but the lives of men are but a quarter of that time. When a mermaid dies we become mere foam to cap the waves – just an added sparkle on the water, but that is all. With men it's different: they possess a spirit soul that rises up to fly among the stars and lives forever in a heavenly kingdom.'

'Oh, if only it could be like that for me,' said the little mermaid. 'I would gladly give my three hundred years for just one day as a human being – to walk among their forests and explore their land.'

An anxious look flickered across her grandmother's face. 'No little one, you should not wish for such a thing. Our lives are happy here in the ocean but men have burdens we could not bear.'

'But will I never see the heavenly land, Grandmama? Will I just become drifting foam and never feel the warm sun on my face again? Is there nothing I can do to become human?'

Her grandmother took her hand and said gently: 'The only way, my child, is for a man to love you more than his own life; when his every thought is of his love for you; then he will take your hand like this and let his soul pass into you. But, no man could love a mermaid. Your beautiful tail would seem absurd to him, no prettier than that of a fish – they do not see beauty as we do.'

*   *   *

Some time later the little mermaid sat at the foot of the palace wall beneath a fathom of sadness. In despair, her thoughts turned to the sea witch: she must have courage and visit the terrible witch to ask for help. A tremor of fear snaked up her long tail and made her shudder.

She set out and swam to a far-off part of the ocean: it was strange to her and she became afraid. Nothing grew here and the water began to swirl and whirl about her; the colourful plants and the fish had vanished and it became a land of slimy darkness. She came at last to the enchanted forest that surrounded the home of the witch. It was not a forest of trees, but one of giant worm-like creatures that squirmed and oozed, back and forth, in the inky waters. They would trap and hold anything that came within reach of their writhing, sucking arms.

For a moment she feared to go on, but then she tucked her flowing hair tightly in her pearly headband and, with her arms held close to her sides, she sped through the blind, groping branches. All around she saw their wretched spoils: sea chests, barrels and cannon; drowned seamen, waving, ghastly, white-boned shadows; animals from the stricken ships that foundered above, eaten and bleached in their death-grip; and worst of all, the tangled yellow hair of a young mermaid, strangled and swaying in the murky tide.

After what seemed an age of twisting through the evil worms, she suddenly swam into a clearing. It bubbled and dripped with ooze and slime and in the centre the sea-witch had built her house; it was made from the skulls and bones of shipwrecked sailors. There sat the witch and the little mermaid had never seen such ugliness. The witch's bloated body was covered with scales and her hair writhed like a thousand worms. White-bellied eels wriggled about her slimy tail, snails crawled on her face and breasts and in her lap sat a bulging sea-slug.

'I know your wish,' she gurgled. 'It is that of a fool, but I can satisfy your desire, . . . if only to bring you pain.' The witch opened her sticky

mouth and a burbling cackle rose from deep in her throat: her body
shook and shivered and some of the snails fell from her skin.

'A potion will I mix,' went on the witch. 'Drink it and you will have
your stumps, your legs; your tail will split and there they'll be. But
though you will walk and dance like an angel, every footstep will cut
you like a thousand knives and your feet will flow crimson with blood.'
The witch's face grimaced into a smile: 'Then let the prince fall in love
with you!' She paused 'well, do you still wish to walk as a human?'

'Yes, I do,' answered the mermaid nervously, and her thoughts of the handsome young prince gave her added strength.

The evil witch leaned her ugly head closer. 'Remember well, Mermaid,' she hissed. 'Once a human, always a human! You may never be a mermaid again, nor swim, nor see your family and share their lives. Also, should you fail to enchant the prince and he does not take you as his wife and love you truly, then you will never gain an immortal soul. Nor will it end there, for should he take another for his bride, then your heart will break and you will die. Just one night should they spend together and you will turn to foam.'

The little mermaid trembled but she nodded her head in agreement.

'Not so fast, my pretty. What of my reward?' And the sea-witch sneered. 'I demand a high price from you, little thing. I'll have your voice, the sweetest in the ocean, that is my price.'

'But without my voice how can I talk with the prince and win his love?' The little mermaid grew fearful and her eyes grew wide.

The sea-witch was getting impatient and her hair writhed angrily.

'Your body will talk for you; your grace and slender form will charm a human heart. It will be my blood, cut from my veins, that seals the potion and gives it the power you need. But first, I'll have that tongue of yours.' She leant forward and gurgled spitefully.

The witch curled her evil body over a swirling cauldron and the potion was mixed.

The little mermaid took the potion from the witch. It was like crystal clear water. She gave no thanks, she was mute and could neither sing nor speak. She swam quickly away from the dreadful place and turned towards the prince's castle. On her way she passed the sleepy palace of her father. She thought fondly of him, her dear sisters and her loving grandmother. She was full of sadness and raised her fingers to her lips to blow them one last kiss.

*   *   *

She reached the prince's castle just before daybreak; peeped above the pale, moon-kissed waters and swallowed the potion. Instantly, a frightful pain, like a red-hot knife blade, shot through her body and she fainted on to the cool sand of the shore.

The morning sun crept up the sky and as its rays swept over the beach, they warmed her face. She awoke and saw a handsome figure with coal-black eyes standing in front of her: it was the prince. Startled, she looked down at herself; she was naked and her tail was gone, in its

place were slender legs. Nervous and abashed, she covered herself with her golden hair.

'Who are you? How have you come to this place?' asked the prince. The sadness in her deep blue eyes was her only answer for she could not speak. He took her hand to lead her to the castle, but as soon as she stood, the witch's words came back to her. In truth, with each step, her feet were slashed by a thousand knives. She suffered the terrible pain in silence and stepped lightly alongside the prince.

In the castle she was dressed in fine silk and soft muslin. She sat in the court and minstrels played while slave-girls sang. One girl sang so sweetly that the prince applauded loudly and the little mermaid feared his attention would be only for her.

But then the slave-girls started to dance and whirled around the court. The little mermaid stood up and glided out amongst them. The others drew back as she tip-toed and danced lightly to the music: such grace and charm of movement were superb to see. She floated like thistledown and every movement of her delightful body emphasised her exquisite form. On and on she danced and the audience was thrilled. The prince became more and more enchanted but he did not know that with every step she took, a pain to match a razor's slash seared her feet.

'You are a delight!' he cried. 'You will stay with us forever. You are my little foundling' – and he laughed kindly at her.

He took her riding through the deep cedar forests and into the sun-dappled groves of scented pines. Wild herbs filled the air with their heady fragrances and the sky was full of birdsong. They climbed high into the mountains, so high that they were able to look down on to the wispy-white clouds. And all the while her feet were cruelly wounded, yet her love for the prince gave her strength and wherever he led her she smiled and followed.

At night she would climb down the marble staircase and bathe her injured feet in the moon-rippled sea. The cool water eased her pain and she let it trickle through her fingers. Suddenly, she heard singing, it was full of sadness and looking up she saw her sisters far out over the water. They waved to her and told of the sorrow her departure had brought to their lives. Each night after that, they came again, and sometimes brought her grandmother and her father with them. They never ventured close but stood far out across the dark rolling waves.

As the days passed, her love for the prince grew stronger. She would look into his face and search his eyes for love, but all she found was fondness. Why could he not love her and make her his wife? Would she never gain an immortal soul? Alas, the prince loved her as he would a child; she was the gentlest girl he knew and he would kiss her brow.

'Your dear sweet face reminds me of another,' he said. 'Once, long ago, I was shipwrecked and cast upon the shore. It was close to a convent and a girl who studied there, tended me and made me well. It is as though my heart can only love that girl, but I fear I will never see her again.'

The little mermaid sighed and turned her eyes sadly away. 'He does not know that it was I who saved him from the storm,' she thought. 'He does not know that it was I who kissed him tenderly and bore him up in the cruel waves and laid his dear head on the warm white sand. Should he not see her again, then perhaps he will grow to love me one day, instead. I will love him more and pray that day will come.'

* * *

'It's about time the prince found a wife and settled down,' said the king. 'He will be married!'

The news spread quickly round the city, and all, save the prince, were excited by it. His heart was not in it, but he would obey his father's wishes and seek a bride. He went into the castle garden with the little mermaid and took her face in his hands.

'Little foundling,' he murmured. 'My one true love is far away and I

shall never see her again. But I have you always by my side to remind me of her, so come with me and help me find a suitable princess to marry. In truth, should I ever marry, I should choose you, for you are the sweetest, dearest one I know.'

They sailed away and the prince spoke to her of the ocean. She listened attentively but inside she smiled to herself. Even had she been able to speak, she would have remained silent, for she knew more of the

ocean's secrets then he could imagine. After many days the ship sailed to a stop and let slip its great iron anchor. Ashore, the town was bustling. Church bells rang and children sang; banners flew from every flag-pole; grand feasts were laid out; soldiers tramped smartly up and down and polished their buttons, and people danced through the streets in preparation for the wedding of the prince to their lovely princess.

But the princess was not due to arrive until the following day. She had been away, studying, at a convent by the sea!

It was, indeed, the same girl the prince had fallen in love with so long ago. It was she who had found him on the beach and cared for him. When the princess arrived the little mermaid saw that she was, without question, very beautiful. Her long dark hair shone like burnished ebony and her lovely face was as fair as the palest rose petal.

'Oh how happy I am,' cried the prince taking hold of the princess's hand. 'I have found my one true love at last. And you, little foundling, shall share my joy, for no-one loves me more dearly than you.'

The little mermaid knelt and kissed his hand; she held it close to her cheek for a brief moment, her heart was close to breaking and her love for him was like a thousand sorrows. Soon, when he wed, she would die and tumble among the foaming waves.

The day of the wedding arrived and the bells chimed across the land. Inside the great cathedral where the ceremony was taking place, the tall silver candlesticks guttered and glowed on the rich tapestries hung on the walls; the great organ peeled and boomed and a vast crowd was seated to witness the affair. Alone, and kneeling close behind the wedding couple, was the little mermaid. She was dressed in rich robes of crimson silk and gold, but she saw and heard nothing. Her heart was full of love for her lost prince and of tomorrow, when with the dawn, she would die.

As dusk settled, the bride and bridgegroom boarded the great ship the sails were let fly from the yards and it glided out on to the silver-black sea. On the main deck a tent had been raised for the young couple and beneath its scarlet and gold awnings was laid a quilt of the softest down: here the prince and his beautiful bride would sleep that night.

When darkness came the lamps were lit all about the ship and the sailors broke into a merry dance. It was so like that other evening long ago when first the little mermaid had swum to the top of the sea. Now, she danced as never before. Her grace was matchless and her step as light as a butterfly. Her feet were still cut by a thousand knives but she no longer felt the pain: no pain could match the sorrow in her heart.

This was her very last night and her head was full of sad memories. Her dear, beloved prince would never know of her sacrifice: the loss of her voice, her sisters, her father and grandmother, and her constant terrible pain.

When the wedding couple retired for the night, the dancing stopped and the ship became quiet – only the helmsman at his creaking wheel and the little mermaid remained awake. She sat in the shadows high in the prow and watched for the first threads of dawn. Her sisters rose out of the waves and she saw that their heads had been shorn of their long flowing hair. Their oyster-pale faces looked up and were sad. 'The sea-witch will help you, dear sister. You need not die. Here is a dagger she gave us; you must take it and pierce the heart of the prince and let his blood wash over your feet. Then you will have a tail again and can swim with us deep in the sea for the three hundred years that we have. Her price was our hair but we do not care.'

The waves tumbled by and they cried out once more. 'Hurry, dear sister, daybreak is close. Either you or the prince must die before dawn. Quickly, the sun is about to awake.'

The breeze sighed and her sisters disappeared. The little mermaid picked up the dagger and softly drew back the curtain of the tent. The handsome prince and his lovely bride were sleeping peacefully. Kneeling beside him, she leant over and kissed him tenderly on the forehead. Her hand clasped the dagger tight to her breast as she looked down on him; how fine he was, so young and strong. His eyelashes flickered and he stirred. Softly, and very gently, she kissed him farewell and left the tent.

She walked to the rail and flung the dagger as far out as she could into the lightening sea. As it sank, the sea around it turned red, as though stained with the blood from a broken heart.

Grey dawn streaked over the waters to the bounding ship and the wavetops were tinged with the palest pink. The little mermaid turned and looked once more at the sleeping prince, but her dear love's face grew hazy as the mist of death clouded her dying eyes. She threw herself into the surging waves, her body grew light and she became the tossing foam of the sea.

*   *   *

The sun peeped its dish over the lip of the waves and sparkled warmly on the singing foam. The little mermaid no longer felt any pain, nor did she feel death. She could see the gold of the sun and feel the comfort of its warm arms around her. It seemed to be lifting her high into the clear, morning sky. All around her, flying and floating, were the airy forms of a thousand beautiful spirits. They were singing sweetly, but so softly that no human being could hear their voices: it was just like the breeze humming over clear crystal waters and rippling on the warm silver sand. She was as they were, a drifting spirit.

'Where am I?' she said, and her voice was the singing of pearls.

'Little mermaid,' breathed the spirits, 'we are the daughters of the air. You cannot gain your immortal soul without the love of a human being. But, like those of us who still wait, you can gain a soul by goodness and caring for others. Carry the fragrance of flowers to those that are sick; blow hard on the mists to dispel the illness held within; lift up the swallows from below, so that those on earth will marvel at their flight – do all of these things for three hundred years and you will find your soul. Your pain and the pure love of your heart is why you are here.'

The sun was now high and she felt its warmth on her face, then, for the first time, a tear rolled down her lovely cheek.

Down on the sea she saw the ship plunging on; she could hear the seamen waking and calling. The prince and his bride stood by the rail and seemed to know she had returned to the sea. Unseen, she drifted down and kissed him; a zephyr of love brushed his cheek.

Then she flew with the others up into the blue summer sky. 'In three hundred years I will see the heavenly kingdom,' she murmured happily.

'Yes, or sooner still, my child,' whispered the spirits. 'When you drift to the bed of a sleeping child and smile an unseen smile, a year will be saved from the three hundred term, but a single tear adds a day.'

The Beginning of the Armadillos

THIS, O BEST BELOVED, is another story of the High and Far-Off Times. In the very middle of those times was a Stickly-Prickly Hedgehog, and he lived on the banks of the turbid Amazon, eating shelly snails and things. And he had a friend, a Slow-Solid Tortoise, who lived on the banks of the turbid Amazon, eating green lettuces and things. And so *that* was all right, Best Beloved. Do you see?

But also, and at the same time, in those High and Far-Off Times, there was a Painted Jaguar, and he lived on the banks of the turbid Amazon too; and he ate everything that he could catch. When he could not catch deer or monkeys he would eat frogs and beetles; and when he could not catch frogs and beetles he went to his Mother Jaguar, and she told him how to eat hedgehogs and tortoises.

She said to him ever so many times, graciously waving her tail, 'My son, when you find a Hedgehog you must drop him into the water and then he will uncoil, and when you catch a Tortoise you must scoop him out of his shell with your paw.' And so that was all right, Best Beloved.

One beautiful night on the banks of the turbid Amazon, Painted Jaguar found Stickly-Prickly Hedgehog and Slow-and-Solid Tortoise sitting under the trunk of a fallen tree. They could not run away, and so Stickly-Prickly curled himself up into a ball, because he was a Hedgehog, and Slow-and-Solid Tortoise drew in his head and feet into his shell as far as they would go, because he was a Tortoise; and so *that* was all right, Best Beloved. Do you see?

'Now attend to me,' said Painted Jaguar, 'because this is very important. My mother said that when I meet a Hedgehog I am to drop him into the water and then he will uncoil, and when I meet a Tortoise I am to scoop him out of his shell with my paw. Now which of you is Hedgehog and which is Tortoise? because, to save my spots, I can't tell.'

'Are you sure of what your Mummy told you?' said Stickly-Prickly Hedgehog. 'Are you quite sure? Perhaps she said that when you uncoil a Tortoise you must shell him out of the water with a scoop, and when you paw a Hedgehog you must drop him on the shell.'

'Are you sure of what your Mummy told you?' said Slow-and-Solid Tortoise. 'Are you quite sure? Perhaps she said that when you water a Hedgehog you must drop him into your paw, and when you meet a Tortoise you must shell him till he uncoils.'

'I don't think it was at all like that,' said Painted Jaguar, but he felt a little puzzled; 'but, please, say it again more distinctly.'

'When you scoop water with your paw you uncoil it with a Hedgehog,' said Stickly-Prickly. 'Remember that, because it's important.'

'*But*,' said the Tortoise, 'when you paw your meat you drop it into a Tortoise with a scoop. Why can't you understand?'

'You are making my spots ache,' said Painted Jaguar; 'and besides, I didn't want your advice at all. I only wanted to know which of you is Hedgehog and which is Tortoise.'

'I shan't tell you,' said Stickly-Prickly. 'But you can scoop me out of my shell if you like.'

'Aha!' said Painted Jaguar. 'Now I know you're Tortoise. You thought I wouldn't! Now I will.' Painted Jaguar darted out his paddy-paw just as Stickly- Prickly curled himself up, and of course Jaguar's paddy-paw was just filled with prickles. Worse than that, he knocked Stickly-Prickly away and away into the woods and the bushes, where it was too dark to find him.

Then he put his paddy-paw into his mouth, and of course the prickles hurt him worse than ever. As soon as he could speak he said, 'Now I know he isn't Tortoise at all. But' – and then he scratched his head with his un-prickly paw – 'how do I know that this other is Tortoise?'

'But I *am* Tortoise,' said Slow-and-Solid. 'Your mother was quite right. She said that you were to scoop me out of my shell with your paw. Begin.'

'You didn't say she said that a minute ago,' said Painted Jaguar, sucking the prickles out of his paddy-paw. 'You said she said something quite different.'

'Well, suppose you say that I said that she said something quite different, I don't see that it makes any difference; because if she said what you said I said she said, it's just the same as if I said what she said she said. On the other hand, if you think she said that you were to uncoil me with a scoop, instead of pawing me into drops with a shell, I can't help that, can I?'

'But you said you wanted to be scooped out of your shell with my paw,' said Painted Jaguar.

'If you'll think again you'll find that I didn't say anything of the kind. I said that your mother said that you were to scoop me out of my shell,' said Slow-and-Solid.

'What will happen if I do?' said the Jaguar most sniffily and most cautious.

'I don't know, because I've never been scooped out of my shell before; but I tell you truly, if you want to see me swim away you've only got to drop me into the water.'

'I don't believe it,' said Painted Jaguar. 'You've mixed up all the things my mother told me to do with the things that you asked me whether I was sure that she didn't say, till I don't know whether I'm on my head or my painted tail; and now you come and tell me something I *can* understand, and it makes me more mixy than before. My mother told me that I was to drop one of you into the water, and as you seem so anxious to be dropped I think you don't want to be dropped. So jump into the turbid Amazon and be quick about it.'

'I warn you that your Mummy won't be pleased. Don't tell her I didn't tell you,' said Slow-and-Solid.

'If you say another word about what my mother said –' the Jaguar answered, but he had not finished the sentence before Slow-and-Solid quietly dived into the turbid Amazon, swam under water for a long way, and came out on the bank where Stickly-Prickly was waiting for him.

'That was a very narrow escape,' said Stickly-Prickly. 'I don't like Painted Jaguar. What did you tell him that you were?'

Painted Jaguar sucked the prickles from his paw

'I told him truthfully that I was a truthful Tortoise, but he wouldn't believe it, and he made me jump into the river to see if I was, and I was, and he is surprised. Now he's gone to tell his Mummy. Listen to him!'

They could hear Painted Jaguar roaring up and down among the trees and the bushes by the side of the turbid Amazon, till his Mummy came.

'Son, son!' said his mother ever so many times, graciously waving her tail, 'what have you been doing that you shouldn't have done?'

'I tried to scoop something that said it wanted to be scooped out of its shell with my paw, and my paw is full of per-ickles,' said Painted Jaguar.

'Son, son!' said his mother ever so many times, graciously waving her tail, 'by the prickles in your paddy-paw I see that that must have been a Hedgehog. You should have dropped him into the water.'

'I did that to the other thing; and he said he was a Tortoise, and I didn't believe him, and it was quite true, and he has dived under the turbid Amazon, and he won't come up again, and I haven't anything at all to eat, and I think we had better find lodgings somewhere else. They are too clever on the turbid Amazon for poor me!'

'Son, son!' said his mother ever so many times, graciously waving her tail, 'now attend to me and remember what I say. A Hedgehog curls himself up into a ball and his prickles stick out every which way at once. By this you may know the Hedgehog.'

'I don't like this old lady one little bit,' said Stickly-Prickly, under the shadow of a large leaf. 'I wonder what else she knows?'

'A Tortoise can't curl himself up,' Mother Jaguar went on, ever so many times, graciously waving her tail. 'He only draws his head and legs into his shell. By this you may know the Tortoise.'

'I don't like this old lady at all – at all,' said Slow-and-Solid Tortoise. 'Even Painted Jaguar can't forget those directions. It's a great pity that you can't swim, Stickly-Prickly.'

'Don't talk to me,' said Stickly-Prickly. 'Just think how much better it would be if you could curl up. This *is* a mess! Listen to Painted Jaguar.'

Painted Jaguar was sitting on the banks of the turbid Amazon sucking

prickles out of his paw and saying to himself:—

'Can't curl, but can swim –
Slow-Solid, that's him!
Curls up, but can't swim –
Stickly-Prickly, that's him!'

'He'll never forget that this month of Sundays,' said Stickly-Prickly. 'Hold up my chin, Slow-and-Solid. I'm going to try to learn to swim. It may be useful.'

'Excellent!' said Slow-and-Solid; and he held up Stickly-Prickly's chin, while Stickly-Prickly kicked in the waters of the turbid Amazon.

'You'll make a fine swimmer yet,' said Slow-and-Solid. 'Now, if you can unlace my back-plates a little, I'll see what I can do towards curling up. It may be useful.'

Stickly-Prickly helped to unlace Tortoise's back-plates, so that by twisting and straining Slow-and-Solid actually managed to curl up a tiddy wee bit.

'Excellent!' said Stickly-Prickly; 'but I shouldn't do any more just now. It's making you black in the face. Kindly lead me into the water once again and I'll practise that side-stroke which you say is so easy.' And so Stickly-Prickly practised, and Slow-and-Solid swam alongside.

'Excellent!' said Slow-and-Solid. 'A little more practice will make you a regular whale. Now, if I may trouble you to unlace my back and front plates two holes more, I'll try that fascinating bend that you say is so easy. Won't Painted Jaguar be surprised!'

'Excellent!' said Stickly-Prickly, all wet from the turbid Amazon. 'I declare, I shouldn't know you from one of my own family. Two holes, I think, you said? A little more expression, please, and don't grunt quite so much, or Painted Jaguar may hear us. When you've finished, I want to try that long dive which you say is so easy. Won't Painted Jaguar be surprised!'

And so Stickly-Prickly dived, and Slow-and-Solid dived alongside.

'Excellent!' said Slow-and-Solid. 'A leetle more attention to holding your breath and you will be able to keep house at the bottom of the turbid Amazon. Now I'll try that exercise of wrapping my hind legs round my ears which you say is so peculiarly comfortable. Won't Painted Jaguar be surprised!'

'Excellent!' said Stickly-Prickly. 'But it's straining your back-plates a little. They are all overlapping now, instead of lying side by side.'

'Oh, that's the result of exercise,' said Slow-and-Solid. 'I've noticed that your prickles seem to be melting into one another, and that you're growing to look rather more like a pine-cone, and less like a chestnut-burr, than you used to.'

'Am I?' said Stickly-Prickly. 'That comes from my soaking in the water. Oh, Won't Painted Jaguar be surprised!'

They went on with their exercises, each helping the other, till morning came; and when the sun was high they rested and dried themselves. Then they saw that they were both of them quite different from what they had been.

'Stickly-Prickly,' said Tortoise after breakfast, 'I am not what I was yesterday; but I think that I may yet amuse Painted Jaguar.'

'That was the very thing I was thinking just now,' said Stickly-Prickly. 'I think scales are a tremendous improvement on prickles – to say nothing of being able to swim. Oh, *won't* Painted Jaguar be surprised! Let's go and find him.'

By and by they found Painted Jaguar, still nursing his paddy-paw that had been hurt the night before. He was so astonished that he fell three times backward over his own painted tail without stopping.

'Good morning!' said Stickly-Prickly. 'And how is your dear gracious Mummy this morning?'

'She is quite well, thank you,' said Painted Jaguar; 'but you must forgive me if I do not at this precise moment recall your name.'

'That's unkind of you,' said Stickly-Prickly, 'seeing that this time yesterday you tried to scoop me out of my shell with your paw.'

'But you hadn't any shell. It was all prickles,' said Painted Jaguar. 'I know it was. Just look at my paw!'

'You told me to drop into the turbid Amazon and be drowned,' said Slow-and-Solid. 'Why are you so rude and forgetful to-day?'

'Don't you remember what your mother told you?' said Stickly-Prickly,

> 'Can't curl, but can swim –
> Stickly-Prickly, that's him!
> Curls up, but can't swim –
> Slow-Solid, that's him!'

They went on with their exercises, each helping the other

Jaguar's eyes turned cart-wheels in his head

Then they both curled themselves up and rolled round and round Painted Jaguar till his eyes turned truly cart-wheels in his head.

Then he went to fetch his mother.

'Mother,' he said, 'there are two new animals in the woods to-day, and the one that you said couldn't swim, swims, and the one that you said couldn't curl up, curls; and they've gone shares in their prickles, I think, because both of them are scaly all over, instead of one being smooth and the other very prickly; and, besides that, they are rolling round and round in circles, and I don't feel comfy.'

'Son, son!' said Mother Jaguar ever so many times, graciously waving her tail, 'a Hedgehog is a Hedgehog, and can't be anything but a Hedgehog; and a Tortoise is a Tortoise, and can never be anything else.'

'But it isn't a Hedgehog, and it isn't a Tortoise. It's a little bit of both, and I don't know its proper name.'

'Nonsense!' said Mother Jaguar. 'Everything has its proper name. I should call it "Armadillo" till I found out the real one. And I should leave it alone.'

So Painted Jaguar did as he was told, especially about leaving them alone; but the curious thing is that from that day to this, O Best Beloved, no one on the banks of the turbid Amazon has ever called Stickly-Prickly and Slow-and-Solid anything except Armadillo. There are Hedgehogs and Tortoises in other places, of course (there are some in my garden); but the real old and clever kind, with their scales lying lippety-lappety one over the other, like pine-cone scales, that lived on the banks of the turbid Amazon in the High and Far-Off Days, are always called Armadillos, because they were so clever.

*   *   *

So *that*'s all right, Best Beloved. Do you see?

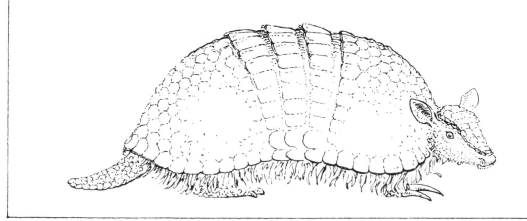

The Astrologer & the Traveller

A CERTAIN astrologer, who was so interested in gazing at the stars that he forgot to watch his way, had the misfortune to fall into a ditch one dark night. His fellow-traveller, who had been watching the road and not the heavens and was therefore unharmed, said, 'Friend, take a lesson from your misfortune and let the stars go quietly on their course in future. It would serve you better if you kept your eyes not on the stars above but on the way you were going.'

Look where you're going.

The Cat & the Mice

A CAT who had grown feeble with age, and was no longer able to hunt mice as she had done in her younger days, thought of a way to entice them within reach of her paws.

She suspended herself by the hind legs from a peg, thinking that the mice would mistake her for a bag, or for a dead cat at least, and would then venture to come near her.

An old mouse who had looked on, but was wise enough to keep his distance, whispered to a friend, 'Many a bag have I seen in my time, but never one with a cat's head.'

'Hang there, good madam,' said the other to the cat, 'as long as you please, but I will not trust myself within reach of you. *You* are not clever enough for us.'

Wise men will not be fooled by old tricks.

The Dog & the Cock

A DOG and a cock were travelling through a wood when night fell. The dog went to sleep in the hollow at the foot of a tree, and the cock roosted in the branches above.

The cock crowed at his usual hour to welcome the dawn, and his cry awoke a fox who lived nearby and who hurried to the tree, thinking he would find himself a meal. When he saw the cock he began to praise his voice and begged the bird to come down from the tree so that he could congratulate him properly.

'I will come down,' said the cock, seeing through the fox's plan, 'if you will first ask the porter below to open the door.'

The fox, not suspecting the trick, did as he was told. When the dog awoke he soon put an end to the fox, and he and the cock journeyed on.

Meet cunning with cunning.

The Frog Prince

LONG AGO THERE LIVED A KING and queen who had a very beautiful daughter. She was, however, very selfish and thought only of herself. Nothing in the palace held her interest for long and she was often very bored.

One day all this changed when the king gave her a present. It was a golden ball and such was the princess's delight it became her favourite toy. She would play all day in the palace garden, throwing the ball high into the air and catching it as it fell back down to her.

She seemed never to tire of her game until, one bright sunny morning, she skipped out of the garden and wandered into the nearby wood. Up and up went the golden ball as she sauntered along, and snatch and catch went her delicate hands as the gleaming ball fell down again. Ambling through the trees, she came presently to the banks of a stream that bubbled into a deep pool at her feet. Up once more went the golden ball but, alas, the princess misdirected her throw and the ball fell down with a splash in the middle of the pool. Slowly it sank into the depths and disappeared.

"Humph!" said the princess petulantly and leaning far out over the water she peered into the pool – the ball was nowhere to be seen.

She grew impatient and began to bemoan her loss, getting more cross by the minute. "Oh really! Now what am I to play with? I only like my golden ball and I can't even see it!" She looked again into the deep waters but still she could not see her treasured toy.

"I'd willingly give up all my fine clothes and all my jewels, in fact, everything I own, if only I could get my ball back." Her voice grew angry and she stamped her foot.

Suddenly, as she stood beside the stream pouting, a frog poked his head above the water. "Princess, why do you look so glum?" he asked. "What is the matter? Your temper quite disturbed me."

The princess looked disdainfully at the frog, then she told him what had happened.

"Well," said the frog, "I can help you, but you may keep your fine clothes and all your jewels. In fact, I seek no reward save that you learn to love me and let me live with you; promise that I may eat at your table and sleep on your pillow and I will dive down and fetch your precious toy."

The princess raised her eyebrows scornfully. "What nonsense!" she said. "A frog living with a princess? Whatever next! And that she should *love* him? I do declare!" Then the princess remembered the golden ball and such was her desire to retrieve it that she said to the frog: "Very well, it will be as you wish, I promise."

Instantly the frog disappeared and returned within seconds with the golden ball in his mouth; he laid it at the princess's feet.

She gave a cry of delight and snatched up the ball. Then, quite forgetting the frog and her promise, she ran off towards the palace.

The frog hopped on to a rock and called after her: "Princess, come back! Have you forgotten your promise?" But she was gone, his call was in vain and she did not hear him.

On the following day the king and the queen and the princess sat down to dine. As they did so there came a knocking at the door. Tap, tap, tap! They stopped eating and looked across the room. Tap, tap, tap! There it was again, but this time it was followed by a small croaky voice:

"Open the door my princess dear
It is your own true love stands here.
Remember the promise you made to me,
Beside the pool, beneath the tree."

The princess stood up and strode towards the door.

"A frog, m'lady," said the footman as he opened the door. The princess had quite forgotten her encounter by the woodland pool and she drew back in alarm at the sight of the frog.

"Shut the door," she ordered. "Immediately!"

"Anyone we know?" asked the king, "You seem a trifle alarmed, my dear."

"No! Only a horrid frog!" said the princess. "I lost my ball in a pool and he retrieved it for me. He made me promise to love him; to let him live with me, eat with me and sleep upon my pillow."

The king raised an eyebrow and the queen looked over her spectacles.

"I never dreamed of such a thing happening," went on the princess. "But now he's here to claim his promise."

"Open the door my princess dear
It is your own true love stands here.
Remember the promise you made to me,
Beside the pool, beneath the tree."

The frog was knocking on the door again and the princess bit her lip. The king put down his knife and fork: "I think you ought to let him in," he mused. "After all, a promise is a promise and it seems a bit rude to leave him standing on the doorstep." The princess nodded reluctantly and once more the footman opened the door. "The frog, m'lady," he announced solemnly.

The frog hopped to the princess's side. "Pray lift me up to the chair that I may sit by you." The princess did so.

"And, sweet princess, place your plate a little nearer, that I may eat with you." The princess pushed her plate closer towards the frog. He ate heartily and at last, when he had had his fill, he turned to the princess and

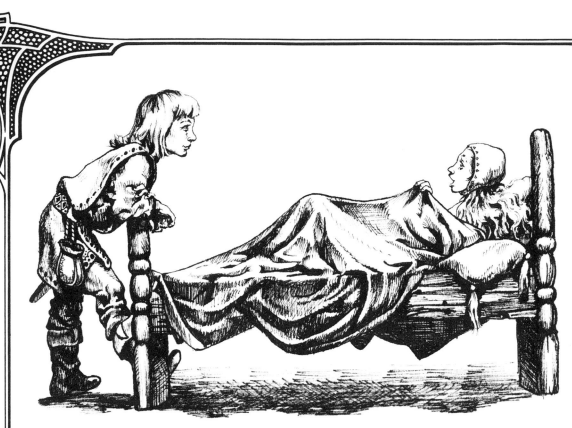

said: "Splendid! Now I am tired. Pray carry me to your bedchamber that I may sleep on your soft feather pillow."

The princess took a deep breath, picked up the frog and walked from the room. She went to her bedchamber and placed the frog beside her on her silken pillow. In the twinkle of an eye he fell into a deep peaceful slumber.

The next morning, when the princess woke up, the frog was gone.

"Thank goodness!" she said. "Now perhaps he will trouble me no more." But she was mistaken: that very same night she heard once more the tap, tap, tap at her door. When she opened it the frog hopped in and slept again on her pillow.

On the third night the same thing happened again, but this time, as dawn crept into the bedchamber, the frog was nowhere to be seen – he had vanished! The princess opened her eyes and turned to see if the frog was lying next to her on her pillow. Then, looking round, her mouth dropped open in surprise for, instead of a frog, a handsome prince stood smiling down at her from the foot of her bed. Noting his good looks and fine clothes, the princess regained her composure and smiled at him demurely.

He began to speak and his voice was soft and gentle. He told a strange tale of a wicked witch who had cast a spell on him, transforming him into a frog. The spell was such that he would forever have the form of a frog unless a princess allowed him to spend three nights on her pillow. "Now," said the prince. "You have broken the spell and by so doing have returned me to my true form." He smiled and took her hand. "Even as a frog I grew to love you, for I had never seen such beauty as yours. Now my love for you is true and my thanks eternal. My greatest wish is that we should marry and live forever in my father's kingdom."

All the time the prince had been speaking a strange warmth had been creeping into the princess's heart. Somehow she felt different: she no longer felt cross at the world and its ways, nor did she feel bored.

"Perhaps," she murmured softly. "There are spells we are not aware of, perhaps these, too, have been broken." She looked up into the prince's dark eyes. Already she felt a deep love for him and she gave her assent to his wish.

All was arranged for the marriage and a fine carriage was drawn up in front of the palace. Six white horses bobbed their heads and waited to take the happy couple away to their new home. The king and queen beamed with happiness, as did the servants – all, that is, except the footmen who were much too important to smile on duty.

The prince led his beautiful bride down the wide sweeping steps and gently took her elbow to assist her into the carriage. But, at the last moment, he hesitated: releasing the handle on the door, he tapped lightly on the coachwork panel.

> "I'll open the door my princess dear
> It is your true love standing here."

The princess laughed and reaching up on tip-toes, kissed him.

45

The Emperor's New Clothes

LONG AGO THERE LIVED AN EMPEROR who only cared about clothes. He spent each and every day dressing up in the finest robes. He was never seen in the same clothes from one hour to the next. His thoughts were on shoes not soldiers, coats not councils, tunics not taxes and gloves instead of governments. People got quite used to his ways and in their talk, instead of saying: 'God's in his heaven, so all is right' they would say: 'The emperor's in his wardrobe, things must be fine.'

The town was large and prosperous, the townsfolk busied themselves about their trade and, all in all, they were very happy. Visitors came and went, buying and selling this and that, or just admiring the town itself. One day, however, two visitors arrived who were very different – they were cheats and tricksters.

They set up shop as weavers of fine cloth and put about their tale: they could, they said, weave a cloth of the most marvellous quality; of the most diverse variety of pattern and colour. The cloth was also special in another way, it could only be seen by the cleverest, noblest, most wise and fitting of people. To those of lesser character and with stupid heads, it would remain invisible.

The word soon spread throughout the town and, as would be expected, the news soon reached the emperor. 'Ah, that cloth I would dearly like to see,' he thought. 'And, . . .' he preened in front of his mirror. 'I shall also be able to see who among my court is clever and who is stupid.'

Straightaway he sent for the weavers. Money was no object: he would have some of the cloth prepared for himself without delay and he paid the weavers handsomely in advance for their services. They asked for gold and silver threads to work into the cloth, and perhaps some precious stones for decoration. Nothing was denied them, although

these items were never seen again. The weavers started work. They set up their loom and sat all day and night weaving away.

The emperor waited and waited. 'When will they finish weaving my cloth?' he thought. But despite his impatience about the progress of the work, the thought of not being able to see the cloth bothered him greatly. 'If I can't see it, I will be thought stupid and that will never do. I must send someone else to find out how things are going.'

He summoned his prime minister, instructed him of his duties, and sent him on his way.

The prime minister did as he was bid but when he entered the weaver's shop he couldn't believe his eyes. The loom was empty!

'But, . . . where is, . . .' he stammered, but stopped himself just in time. He dare not say more lest he be thought an idiot and be thrown out of office. He blinked, rubbed his eyes and looked again. The loom was still empty; he could still not see any cloth. He was so confused he just stood there with his mouth open.

'You may well gasp,' said the weavers. 'Isn't it the finest cloth you have ever seen? Here, feel the fine quality. Look at the beauty of the pattern.' As if he was holding a piece of cloth the weaver held out his empty hands. The minister was now so shocked that all he could do was pretend. He rubbed his thumb and finger together as if feeling the cloth. 'It's the finest, the best, the most beautiful I've, . . . ever . . . seen,' he mumbled. 'The emperor will be delighted.'

The prime minister took note of all the things the weavers had said: which pattern went where, how the colour was arranged, and, of course, their demands for more money.

'Materials are so expensive, good sir,' they whined. 'We will surely need more gold and silver thread in order to complete the cloth.'

More days passed and once again the emperor sent for news of the cloth. This time he sent a clerk to check the weaver's progress.

'Sir, I can't believe it myself, some days,' the oily weavers bowed and scraped. 'Is that not, without doubt, the finest piece of cloth you've ever seen?' The clerk could not see anything but he chose to remain silent. He could see the empty loom but not the cloth. Then, recovering his senses he said: 'Of course, of course. Without question. It is superb!' The poor clerk left as quickly as he could, feeling very upset. 'Can I really be that stupid,' he asked as he hurried back to the emperor's palace.

The marvellous cloth became the talk of the town and at last the emperor set off to see it for himself. He took with him his ministers and clerks, his council and the court and his men-at-arms. 'They shall see it too,' he said.

The prime minister was the first to break the silence in the weaver's shop. 'What do you think, Your Majesty? Isn't it superb!'

The emperor gulped. 'Are my eyes deceiving me,' he thought. 'Where is the cloth? I can't see a single thread. Surely *I'm* not stupid – I must pretend that I can see it. No-one must know that I can't, otherwise I'll be thrown off the throne.' The weavers smiled and bobbed and bowed in front of the emperor.

'It's wonderful!' he said.

'And look at the fantastic colours!' added the clerk. The rest of the

gathering crowded forward: they could see nothing but each believed that all around him could. 'Oh yes! Such pattern! What texture! What fine quality!' They heaped their praises on the unseen cloth. The emperor, they said, must surely order a suit of robes for the coming town procession. They left, but not before the weavers had again been rewarded for their labours.

As the day of the procession drew near the light in the weaver's shop burned long into the night. The townsfolk peered through the windows and were amazed. There sat an empty loom, yet the weavers wound invisible cloth from it; they carried invisible cloth to their cutting table; they flashed their scissors through the air and then sat, cross-legged, sewing at nothing.

At last the word came that the clothes were finished. Down came the clerks, and the court and the council, and the men-at-arms – at their head strode the emperor.

The weavers stood with hands behind backs. 'What do you think, Your Majesty,' they chorused. They took hold of the air and held up the air and showed the air to the emperor. 'Notice the detail on the shirt and trousers,' they chirped. 'See the trim of the coat and the fall of the train. Isn't it just what His Majesty had hoped for?'

The emperor gulped but all around him his courtiers mumbled their approval.

'Now, if Your Majesty will remove the, er, . . . fine suit he is wearing at present, we will re-attire him.'

His imperial pink majesty stood before the long mirror. The weavers lifted his arms and slipped on a shirt he could not see. He stepped into trousers he could not see and raised his chin while a cloak he could not see was buckled under his throat.

'Oh, what a perfect fit! And so suited to Your Majesty's fine bearing.' The courtiers clasped their hands together and leant back in admiration. None would dare declare that, as far as they could see, the emperor wore nothing. Nothing at all!

The great procession started. Leading the way, striding out quite proudly, was the emperor. Indeed, his clothes were as light as a feather, he could not even feel them. Behind him came two footmen holding their finger tips together in the air. They looked a little worried; each pretending to carry the emperor's train but neither of them would dare to say that he could neither see nor feel it.

Through the town they went, and people lined the streets and cheered. None there could see the emperor's clothes, yet none would dare speak of it for fear of being thought stupid.

'Bravo!' they called. 'What splendid clothes! What style! What taste! How well His Majesty looks! Such finery!'

But then a small voice was heard among the crowd. 'But he has nothing on!' It was a child.

The people close to the child hushed him, but thought: 'The child is right' He has nothing on!' The words spread throughout the crowd.

'But he has nothing on!'

The poor emperor trudged on. 'How stupid have I been. They are right,' he thought. 'I do have nothing on!'

The Horse & the Stag

A LONG time ago a wild horse lived and grazed in a vast green meadow. The meadow was wide and provided the sweetest grass for feeding – no other animal came there and the horse had it all to himself.

One day, much to the dismay of the horse, an antlered stag leapt into the meadow and, trampling around, trod down much of the horse's fine grass. This greatly annoyed the horse and, unable to prevent the stag's destructive behaviour, he galloped away towards a man who was passing close by.

'Sir,' said the horse, 'please stop and help me to punish that intruder before my entire grazing is spoiled.'

The man looked back towards the stag who was still leaping about wildly, trampling and stomping; then turning to the horse he said, 'Yes, I will help you to be revenged, but first you must let me place a bit in your mouth for a bridle, and a saddle on your back so that I may mount you. I will provide weapons and then, together, we will be able to overpower that wilful beast.'

The horse agreed eagerly and all was made ready; then with the man mounted on his back he gave chase to the stag. The hunt was short and the stag was soon overcome and slain, which pleased the horse.

He turned to thank the man for his aid but found he could not move his head freely; there was no answer except a sharp tug on the bridle attached to the hard bit in his mouth.

'No need to thank me, horse,' said the man, 'it is I who should thank you. Until now I did not know how useful you could be, nor how swiftly you could carry me across the land. Your revenge has been rewarding to me for in future I will keep you as my servant.'

Thus from that day to this the horse has been the slave of man.

Revenge is dearly bought at the price of liberty.

The Lion & the Mouse

ALONG while ago in a country far away there lived a fierce and handsome lion. Once, when weary from hunting and faint from the heat of the day, he returned home to his lair and fell into a deep sleep.

Whilst he slept a small mouse passed by and, not looking where he was going, absent-mindedly wandered into the lion's den. His tiny eyes slowly grew accustomed to the gloom and, as they did so, they opened wider and wider – there, confronting him, was the most fearsome creature he had ever seen. For a brief moment he was rooted to the spot in terror, then in a sudden panic he sprang towards the door. In so doing he stumbled and tripped over the lion's nose and woke him.

The frightened mouse scrambled frantically to pick himself up, but the lion's great paw clapped down upon him. He thought his end had surely come. And it is true the lion would have made a meal of him, there and then, had not the mouse found his voice.

'Spare me, mighty one,' he pleaded. 'I have accidentally offended you, I know, but your paw is too honourable to stain with the blood of so insignificant a prey.'

The great lion looked quizzically at the mouse and considered the matter without speaking. Then, as the mouse lay there trembling, he lifted his paw and allowed his tiny prisoner to go free. Hardly believing his good fortune, the mouse scampered away with hardly a backward look, fleeing as fast as he could out into the forest.

Now it happened that not long afterwards, the lion was once again hunting in the woods and by mischance fell into a trap set by some hunters. He struggled desperately to escape from the net entangling him but to no avail. Angry and with no hope of freedom, he set up a mighty roar that filled the whole forest with its echo.

Far away the mouse heard the roar and ran quickly to discover its source. At last, in a small clearing, he found the captive lion, which he recognized as the same one who had spared his life and set him free. Without more ado, and showing no fear at all, the mouse ran out and began to nibble at the cords that tightly bound the lion. In a short while the mouse's sharp teeth severed the net and the noble beast was released from his captivity.

Kindness given, to great or humble,
is seldom wasted.

How the Camel got his Hump

NOW THIS IS THE NEXT TALE, and it tells how the Camel got his big hump.

In the beginning of years, when the world was so new-and-all, and the Animals were just beginning to work for Man, there was a Camel, and he lived in the middle of a Howling Desert because he did not want to work; and besides, he was a Howler himself. So he ate sticks and thorns and tamarisks and milkweed and prickles, most 'scruciating idle; and when anybody spoke to him he said 'Humph!' Just 'Humph!' and no more.

Presently the Horse came to him on Monday morning, with a saddle on his back and a bit in his mouth, and said, 'Camel, O Camel, come out and trot like the rest of us.'

'Humph!' said the Camel; and the Horse went away and told the Man.

Presently the Dog came to him, with a stick in his mouth, and said, 'Camel, O Camel, come and fetch and carry like the rest of us.'

'Humph!' said the Camel; and the Dog went away and told the Man.

Presently the Ox came to him, with the yoke on his neck, and said, 'Camel, O Camel, come and plough like the rest of us.'

'Humph!' said the Camel; and the Ox went away and told the Man.

At the end of the day the Man called the Horse and the Dog and the Ox together, and said, 'Three, O Three, I'm very sorry for you (with the world so new-and-all); but that Humph-thing in the Desert can't work, or he would have been here by now, so I am going to leave him alone, and you must work double-time to make up for it.'

That made the Three very angry (with the world so new-and-all), and they held a palaver, and an *indaba*, and a *punchayet*, and a pow-wow on the edge of the Desert; and the Camel came chewing milkweed *most* 'scruciating idle, and laughed at them. Then he said 'Humph!' and went away again.

Presently there came along the Djinn in charge of All Deserts, rolling in a cloud of dust (Djinns always travel that way because it is Magic), and he

And the Camel came chewing . . . most 'scruciating idle

stopped to palaver and pow-wow with the Three.

'Djinn of All Deserts,' said the Horse, '*is* it right for any one to be idle, with the world so new-and-all?'

'Certainly not,' said the Djinn.

'Well,' said the Horse, 'there's a thing in the middle of your Howling Desert (and he's a Howler himself) with a long neck and long legs, and he hasn't done a stroke of work since Monday morning. He won't trot.'

'Whew!' said the Djinn, whistling, 'that's my Camel, for all the gold in Arabia! What does he say about it?'

'He says "Humph!"' said the Dog; 'and he won't fetch and carry.'

'Does he say anything else?'

'Only "Humph!"; and he won't plough,' said the Ox.

'Very good,' said the Djinn. 'I'll humph him if you will kindly wait a minute.'

The Djinn rolled himself up in his dust-cloak, and took a bearing across the desert, and found the Camel most 'scruciatingly idle, looking at his own reflection in a pool of water.

'My long and bubbling friend,' said the Djinn, 'what's this I hear of your doing no work, with the world so new-and-all?'

'Humph!' said the Camel.

The Djinn sat down, with his chin in his hand, and began to think a Great Magic, while the Camel looked at his own reflection in the pool of water.

'You've given the Three extra work ever since Monday morning, all on account of your 'scruciating idleness,' said the Djinn; and he went on thinking Magics, with his chin in his hand.

'Humph!' said the Camel.

'I shouldn't say that again if I were you,' said the Djinn; 'you might say it once too often. Bubbles, I want you to work.'

And the Camel said 'Humph!' again; but no sooner had he said it than he saw his back, that he was so proud of, puffing up and puffing up into a great big lolloping humph.

'Do you see that?' said the Djinn. 'That's your very own humph that you've brought upon your very own self by not working. To-day is Thursday, and you've done no work since Monday, when the work began. Now you are going to work.'

'How can I,' said the Camel, 'with this humph on my back?'

'That's made a-purpose,' said the Djinn, 'all because you missed those three days. You will be able to work now for three days without eating, because you can live on your humph; and don't you ever say I never did anything for you. Come out of the Desert and go to the Three, and behave. Humph yourself!'

And the Camel humphed himself, humph and all, and went away to join the Three. And from that day to this the Camel always wears a humph (we call it 'hump' now, not to hurt his feelings); but he has never yet caught up with the three days that he missed at the beginning of the world, and he has never yet learned how to behave.

The Fox
& the Monkey

A MONKEY once danced in an assembly of the beasts, and so greatly pleased them by his performance that they straight-away elected him their king.

A fox who envied him the honour, having discovered a piece of meat lying in a trap, led the monkey to the titbit and said:

'Look! I have found this store, but have not used it. It is not for the subject to lay claim to a treasure trove; the king himself should take it.'

The monkey approached carelessly and was caught in the trap, whereupon he accused the fox of leading him into the snare.

The fox replied, 'O monkey, can it be that you, with so simple a mind, could rule as king over all the beasts?'

The simple are easily deceived.

The Monkey & the Buffalo

M ANY years later when the monkey was much wiser he danced again before all the beasts. Once more he greatly pleased them and was loudly applauded. The buffalo, however, was piqued by these attentions and seeking fame himself he stepped forward to dance in front of the animals.

He cavorted and pranced, but his dance was so clumsy and so utterly absurd that all the assembled beasts at first laughed at his foolish antics and then rose up in disgust and drove him out of their sight.

Do not step beyond your abilities.

The Sleeping Princess

HERE WAS ONCE A KINGDOM FAR AWAY ruled by a very kind king and his equally kind wife, the queen. They lived in a fine palace of courtyards and colonnades, ballrooms and balconies, turrets and terraces and all day long it hustled and bustled as people went about their business. Although there was much scurrying to-and-fro the king and queen were often lonely as they had no children.

One day, while the queen was walking in the palace garden, she passed close by a small stream. To her surprise a fish suddenly poked its head above the gurgling water and spoke to her.

"Good morning, your majesty," he said cheerfully. "Please, do not look so sad. If you wish for a child your wish will soon be granted – you are to have a baby girl of your own."

As quickly as he had appeared, so the fish vanished, leaving the astonished queen standing there open-mouthed. However, the fish was right, and not long after, the queen gave birth to a beautiful baby girl.

The king was so delighted with his enchanting new daughter that he decided to give a great feast in her honour. Invitations were despatched to the far corners of the kingdom – to all his friends and relations and the noblemen of the court. He also wished to invite all the fairies who lived within the magic glades of his forest. Their powers would bestow good fortune on his child throughout her life.

But, to the king's dismay, he had invited so many people that he was left with only twelve golden dishes for the fairies to eat from, and there were thirteen fairies! One of them would have to be left out.

The day of the feast arrived and one by one the twelve invited fairies came to the palace. Each had brought a special gift for the princess: one brought virtue, one brought beauty, another brought riches, and yet another brought wisdom – and so on until the little princess was endowed with all that is excellent in the world. Eleven of the fairies had bestowed their gifts when suddenly a dark figure stepped forward from the crowd. It was the thirteenth fairy who had not been invited to the feast. She was cold with anger and her eyes blazed with revenge at being slighted. She began to speak and her voice was heavy with malice.

"This princess will thrive, but not for long, just until the day of her fifteenth year. Then, she will be wounded by a spindle and she will die!"

The assembled gathering was stunned and silent. To wish for such an evil thing to happen was unthinkable. But then another figure stepped forward – it was the twelfth fairy who had not yet given her gift to the princess.

"Let me now give my gift," she said in a soft voice. "I cannot stop this evil spell from taking its course, but be assured, the princess will not die. Should she be injured by the spindle she will fall asleep, but alas, her sleep will last for one hundred years."

The king was beside himself with fear and gave orders that every spindle in the land be destroyed immediately lest the threat come to pass. Not one spindle must remain to injure his precious daughter.

The years passed and the fairies' gifts were fruitful. The princess grew more beautiful each day; she was well-mannered and amiable; her kindness was beyond compare, and her wisdom and honesty made all who knew her love her more.

At last, however, the day of her fifteenth birthday arrived. The king and queen had left the palace to search for a special present for their daughter and she was left alone for the day. Feeling a little bored she wandered through the halls and chambers of the palace seeking amusement. She discovered rooms she had never seen before and came at last to the foot of a winding staircase that twisted up to the top of a tower. She daintily ascended and as she climbed the stairs it began to get dark and gloomy. At last she reached the top and there, set in the keyhole of an iron-studded door, was a golden key. The princess reached out and turned it and the door sprang open. In front of her sat a little old lady quietly spinning at her wheel.

"Why, good mother, how came you to be here?" asked the princess pleasantly. "And what is it that you do with so pretty a wheel?"

The old woman smiled and rested from her work. "I am spinning, my child. Do you not know how it is done?" And she rose and passed the spindle to the princess.

"How enchantingly the wheel spins," said the princess, laughing happily, but hardly had she uttered the words when she felt a sharp pain in her finger. The spindle had sorely pricked her – instantly she slumped from the stool and fell lifeless to the floor.

The prophecy had come true. However, the princess was not dead but only sleeping, but then an even stranger thing took place. The king and queen had just returned to the palace and had begun to search for their daughter: at the very moment the spindle had pierced her finger they too, fell asleep. So did the courtiers and the cooks, the footmen and the guards, the kitchen cats and the courtyard dogs – in fact, every living thing within the palace fell into a deep slumber.

Time passed by and a great thicket of tangled thorns grew up around the palace completely hiding it from view. No passers-by could see beyond the dense wall of briar and thorns and in time the palace and its occupants were almost forgotten.

A few old men remembered the story of the beautiful princess who slept within the enchanted castle and passed the tale down to their sons. Many princes and noblemen had heard the same tale and sought to find this unknown beauty within her sleeping castle – but all had failed. Some had given up their search at the first sight of the tangled bushes and vicious spiny thorns. Others had struggled through for a few yards only to find themselves trapped, and, snared within the thicket, had perished where they lay.

Many more years passed and there came to those parts a king's son. He had been hunting close by and stopped to spend the night at a lonely cottage. The old man who lived there did not have many visitors and was pleased to have some company to talk with. He told the prince about the hidden palace, lingering over the story, stopping and starting and puffing on his old pipe. The prince listened patiently and when the old man described how beautiful the princess was, his eyes opened wide with interest.

"I think, old man, that I will seek out this maiden, and if she is as fair as you tell, then she will be my wife."

The old man drew in his breath and laid down his pipe. He also remembered his grandfather's warning: of many such daring adventures and many princes and noblemen who had died in their efforts to seek the sleeping beauty.

"Take care, my son," he said kindly. "Not one brave man has yet lived to tell of the maiden's beauty. The thorns are so thick that all have been ensnared and perished." The old man was fearful for the young prince's life and went on: "Pay no heed to my words. It is just an old man's foolish story."

The prince was not deceived and made up his mind to seek out the enchanted castle as soon as dawn broke. He bade farewell to the old man and set out on his way. It was three whole days and three nights before he came upon the wall of thorns. There he stopped and set up his camp to wait for morning, thinking long into the night on how best to cut his way through the spiny barrier.

By great good fortune the morning of the fourth day marked the end of the one hundred year curse. When the prince opened his eyes the wall of thorns had vanished. In their place was a wild abundant growth of sweetly perfumed flowers. True, they grew to a great height and were sprouting thickly in all directions but they would not prevent the prince's progress. The prince passed through them with ease but as he neared the castle the forest of blooms closed up behind him as thick as ever, leaving no trace of his path.

At last he felt the solid stones of the courtyard beneath his feet. He could hardly believe his eyes: there were the sleeping dogs, while on the roof slept doves with their heads beneath their wings. In the kitchen sleeping cooks rested by their pots, and guards and footmen lounged, snoring, in all the halls and chambers. He came upon the two great thrones and saw the sleeping king and queen – nothing stirred, all was quiet. He wandered on through the silent castle and every breath he took sounded in his ears. At last he came to a staircase leading to the upper floors of the palace and he bounded up without delay. At the far end of a long passage he came to the door of a small bedchamber. He entered and there was the maiden sleeping peacefully on her silken pillows. She was indeed of such serene beauty that he could not take his eyes off her. He bent and gently kissed her lips.

Instantly the princess opened her eyes and looking up, she smiled at him. He took her hand and led her from the chamber. The palace yawned and all about them people began to stretch and wake up. The king and queen, the courtiers and the cooks, the guards and the footmen, the dogs and the cats and even the pigeons – all were waking as if they had fallen asleep only the previous day.

The spell was broken. The prince declared his love for the princess and she, in turn, agreed to be his wife. The king called for a great feast to be held and from that day on they lived happily ever after.

The Cat that Walked by Himself

**H**EAR AND ATTEND and listen; for this befell and behappened and became and was, O my Best Beloved, when the Tame animals were wild. The Dog was wild, and the Horse was wild, and the Cow was wild, and Sheep was wild, and the Pig was wild – as wild as wild could be – and they walked in the Wet Wild Woods by their wild lones. But the wildest of all the wild animals was the Cat. He walked by himself, and all places were alike to him.

Of course the Man was wild too. He was dreadfully wild. He didn't even begin to be tame till he met the Woman, and she told him that she did not like living in his wild ways. She picked out a nice dry Cave, instead of a heap of wet leaves, to lie down in; and she strewed clean sand on the floor; and she lit a nice fire of wood at the back of the Cave; and she hung a dried wild-horse skin, tail-down, across the opening of the Cave; and she said, 'Wipe your feet, dear, when you come in, and now we'll keep house.'

That night, Best Beloved, they ate wild sheep roasted on the hot stones, and flavoured with wild garlic and wild pepper; and wild duck stuffed with wild rice and wild fenugreek and wild coriander; and marrow-bones of wild oxen; and wild cherries, and wild grenadillas. Then the Man went to sleep in front of the fire ever so happy; but the Woman sat up, combing her hair. She took the bone of the shoulder of mutton – the big flat blade-bone – and she looked at the wonderful marks on it, and she threw more wood on the fire, and she made a Magic. She made the First Singing Magic in the world.

Out in the Wet Wild Woods all the wild animals gathered together where they could see the light of the fire a long way off, and they wondered what it meant.

Then Wild Horse stamped with his wild foot and said, 'O my Friends and O my Enemies, why have the Man and the Woman made that great light in that great Cave, and what harm will it do us?'

Wild Dog lifted up his wild nose and smelled the smell of the roast mutton, and said, 'I will go up and see and look, and say; for I think it is

Then Wild Horse stamped with his great wild foot

good. Cat, come with me.'

'Nenni!' said the Cat. 'I am the Cat who walks by himself, and all places are alike to me. I will not come.'

'Then we can never be friends again,' said Wild Dog, and he trotted off to the Cave. But when he had gone a little way the Cat said to himself, 'All places are alike to me. Why should I not go too and see and look and come away at my own liking?' So he slipped after Wild Dog softly, very softly, and hid himself where he could hear everything.

When Wild Dog reached the mouth of the Cave he lifted up the dried horse-skin with his nose and sniffed the beautiful smell of the roast mutton, and the Woman, looking at the blade-bone, heard him, and laughed, and said, 'Here comes the first. Wild Thing out of the Wild Woods, what do you want?'

Wild Dog said, 'O my Enemy and Wife of my Enemy, what is this that smells so good in the Wild Woods?'

Then the Woman picked up a roasted mutton-bone and threw it to Wild Dog, and said, 'Wild Thing out of the Wild Woods, taste and try.' Wild Dog gnawed the bone, and it was more delicious than anything he had ever tasted, and he said, 'O my Enemy and Wife of my Enemy, give me another.'

The Woman said, 'Wild Thing out of the Wild Woods, help my Man to hunt through the day and guard this Cave at night, and I will give you as many roast bones as you need.'

'Ah!' said the Cat, listening. 'This is a very wise Woman, but she is not so wise as I am.'

Wild Dog crawled into the Cave and laid his head on the Woman's lap, and said, 'O my Friend and Wife of my Friend, I will help your Man to hunt through the day, and at night I will guard your Cave.'

'Ah!' said the Cat, listening. 'That is a very foolish Dog.' And he went back through the Wet Wild Woods waving his wild tail, and walking by his wild lone. But he never told anybody.

When the Man waked up he said, 'What is Wild Dog doing here?' And the Woman said, 'His name is not Wild Dog any more, but the First Friend, because he will be our friend for always and always. Take him with you when you go hunting.'

Next night the Woman cut great green armfuls of fresh grass from the water-meadows, and dried it before the fire, so that it smelt like new-mown hay, and she sat at the mouth of the Cave and plaited a halter out of horse-hide, and she looked at the shoulder-of-mutton bone – at the big broad blade-bone – and she made a Magic. She made the Second Singing Magic in the world.

Out in the Wild Woods all the wild animals wondered what had happened to Wild Dog, and at last Wild Horse stamped with his foot and said, 'I will go and see and say why Wild Dog has not returned. Cat, come with me.'

'Nenni!' said the Cat. 'I am the Cat who walks by himself, and all places are alike to me. I will not come.' But all the same he followed Wild Horse softly, very softly, and hid himself where he could hear everything.

When the Woman heard Wild Horse tripping and stumbling on his long mane, she laughed and said, 'Here comes the second. Wild Thing out of the Wild Woods, what do you want?'

Wild Horse said, 'O my Enemy and Wife of my Enemy, where is Wild Dog?'

The Woman laughed, and picked up the blade-bone and looked at it, and said, 'Wild Thing out of the Wild Woods, you did not come here for Wild Dog, but for the sake of this good grass.'

And Wild Horse, tripping and stumbling on his long mane, said, 'That is true; give it me to eat.'

The Woman said, 'Wild Thing out of the Wild Woods, bend your wild head and wear what I give you, and you shall eat the wonderful grass three times a day.'

Wild Cow promised milk in exchange for the wonderful grass

'Ah!' said the Cat, listening. 'This is a clever Woman, but she is not so clever as I am.'

Wild Horse bent his wild head, and the Woman slipped the plaited-hide halter over it, and Wild Horse breathed on the Woman's feet and said, 'O my Mistress, and Wife of my Master, I will be your servant for the sake of the wonderful grass.'

'Ah!' said the Cat, listening. 'That is a very foolish Horse.' And he went back through the Wet Wild Woods, waving his wild tail and walking by his wild lone. But he never told anybody.

When the Man and the Dog came back from hunting, the Man said, 'What is Wild Horse doing here?' And the Woman said, 'His name is not Wild Horse any more, but the First Servant, because he will carry us from place to place for always and always and always. Ride on his back when you go hunting.'

Next day, holding her wild head high that her wild horns should not catch in the wild trees, Wild Cow came up to the Cave, and the Cat followed, and hid himself just the same as before; and everything happened just the same as before; and the Cat said the same things as before; and when Wild Cow had promised to give her milk to the Woman every day in exchange for the wonderful grass, the Cat went back through the Wet Wild Woods waving his wild tail and walking by his wild lone, just the same as before. But he never told anybody. And when the Man and the Horse and the Dog came home from hunting and asked the same questions same as before, the Woman said, 'Her name is not Wild Cow any more, but the Giver of Good Food. She will give us the warm white milk for always and always and always, and I will take care of her while you and the First Friend and the First Servant go hunting.'

Next day the Cat waited to see if any other Wild Thing would go up to the Cave, but no one moved in the Wet Wild Woods, so the Cat walked there by himself; and he saw the Woman milking the Cow, and he saw the light of the fire in the Cave, and he smelt the smell of the warm white milk.

Cat said, 'O my Enemy and Wife of my Enemy, where did Wild Cow go?'

The Woman laughed and said, 'Wild Thing out of the Wild Woods, go back to the Woods again, for I have braided up my hair, and I have put away the magic blade-bone, and we have no more need of either friends or servants in our Cave.'

Cat said, 'I am not a friend, and I am not a servant. I am the Cat who walks by himself, and I wish to come into your Cave.'

Woman said, 'Then why did you not come with First Friend on the first night?'

Cat grew very angry and said, 'Has Wild Dog told tales of me?'

Then the Woman laughed and said, 'You are the Cat who walks by himself, and all places are alike to you. You are neither a friend nor a servant. You have said it yourself. Go away and walk by yourself in all places alike.'

Then Cat pretended to be sorry and said, 'Must I never come into the Cave? Must I never sit by the warm fire? Must I never drink the warm white milk? You are very wise and very beautiful. You should not be cruel even to a Cat.'

Woman said, 'I knew I was wise, but I did not know I was beautiful. So I will make a bargain with you. If ever I say one word in your praise, you may come into the Cave.'

'And if you say two words in my praise?' said the Cat.

'I never shall,' said the Woman, 'but if I say two words in your praise, you may sit by the fire in the Cave.'

'And if you say three words?' said the Cat.

'I never shall,' said the Woman, 'but if I say three words in your praise, you may drink the warm white milk three times a day for always and always and always.'

Then the Cat arched his back and said, 'Now let the Curtain at the mouth of the Cave, and the Fire at the back of the Cave, and the Milk-pots that stand beside the Fire, remember what my Enemy and the Wife of my Enemy has said.' And he went away through the Wet Wild Woods waving his wild tail and walking by his wild lone.

That night when the Man and the Horse and the Dog came home from hunting, the Woman did not tell them of the bargain that she had made with the Cat, because she was afraid that they might not like it.

Cat went far and far away and hid himself in the Wet Wild Woods by his wild lone for a long time till the Woman forgot all about him. Only the Bat – the little upside-down Bat –that hung inside the Cave knew where Cat hid; and every evening Bat would fly to Cat with news of what was happening.

One evening Bat said, 'There is a Baby in the Cave. He is new and pink and fat and small, and the Woman is very fond of him.'

'Ah,' said the Cat, listening. 'But what is the Baby fond of?'

'He is fond of things that are soft and tickle,' said the Bat. 'He is fond of warm things to hold in his arms when he goes to sleep. He is fond of being played with. He is fond of all those things.'

'Ah,' said the Cat, listening. 'Then my time has come.'

Next night Cat walked through the Wet Wild Woods and hid very near the Cave till morning-time, and Man and Dog and Horse went hunting.

The Woman was busy cooking that morning, and the Baby cried and
interrupted. So she carried him outside the Cave and gave him a handful
of pebbles to play with. But still the Baby cried.

Then the Cat put out his paddy paw and patted the Baby on the cheek,
and it cooed; and the Cat rubbed against its fat knees and tickled it under
its fat chin with his tail. And the Baby laughed; and the Woman heard him
and smiled.

Then the Bat – the little upside-down Bat – that hung in the mouth of
the Cave said, 'O my Hostess and Wife of my Host and Mother of my
Host's Son, a Wild Thing from the Wild Woods is most beautifully playing
with your Baby.'

'A blessing on that Wild Thing whoever he may be,' said the Woman,
straightening her back, 'for I was a busy woman this morning and he has
done me a service.'

That very minute and second, Best Beloved, the dried horse-skin
Curtain that was stretched tail-down at the mouth of the Cave fell down –
woosh! – because it remembered the bargain she had made with the Cat;
and when the Woman went to pick it up – lo and behold! – the Cat was
sitting quite comfy inside the Cave.

'O my Enemy and Wife of my Enemy and Mother of my Enemy,' said the Cat, 'it is I: for you have spoken a word in my praise, and now I can sit within the Cave for always and always and always. But still I am the Cat who walks by himself, and all places are alike to me.'

The Woman was very angry, and shut her lips tight and took up her spinning-wheel and began to spin.

But the Baby cried because the Cat had gone away, and the Woman could not hush it, for it struggled and kicked and grew black in the face.

'O my Enemy and Wife of my Enemy and Mother of my Enemy,' said the Cat, 'take a strand of the thread that you are spinning and tie it to your spindle-whorl and drag it along the floor, and I will show you a Magic that shall make your Baby laugh as loudly as he is now crying.'

'I will do so,' said the Woman, 'because I am at my wits' end; but I will not thank you for it.'

She tied the thread to the little clay spindle-whorl and drew it across the floor, and the Cat ran after it and patted it with his paws and rolled head over heels, and tossed it backward over his shoulder and chased it between his hind legs and pretended to lose it, and pounced down upon it again, till the Baby laughed as loudly as it had been crying, and scrambled after the Cat and frolicked all over the Cave till it grew tired and settled down to sleep with the Cat in its arms.

'Now,' said Cat, 'I will sing the Baby a song that shall keep him asleep for an hour.' And he began to purr, loud and low, low and loud, till the Baby fell fast asleep. The Woman smiled as she looked down upon the two of them, and said, 'That was wonderfully done. No question but you are very clever, O Cat.'

*Cat frolicked all over the cave
and the Baby laughed loudly*

That very minute and second, Best Beloved, the smoke of the Fire at the back of the Cave came down in clouds from the roof – *puff!* – because it remembered the bargain she had made with the Cat; and when it had cleared away – lo and behold! – the Cat was sitting quite comfy close to the fire.

'O my Enemy and Wife of my Enemy and Mother of my Enemy,' said the Cat, 'it is I: for you have spoken a second word in my praise, and now I can sit by the warm fire at the back of the Cave for always and always and always. But still I am the Cat who walks by himself, and all places are alike to me.'

Then the Woman was very very angry, and let down her hair and put more wood on the fire and brought out the broad blade-bone of the shoulder of mutton and began to make a Magic that should prevent her from saying a third word in praise of the Cat. It was not a Singing Magic, Best Beloved, it was a Still Magic; and by and by the Cave grew so still that a little wee-wee mouse crept out of a corner and ran across the floor.

'O my Enemy and Wife of my Enemy and Mother of my Enemy,' said the Cat, 'is that little mouse part of your Magic?'

'Ouh! Chee! No indeed!' said the Woman, and she dropped the blade-bone and jumped upon the footstool in front of the fire and braided up her hair very quick for fear that the mouse should run up it.

'Ah,' said the Cat, watching. 'Then the mouse will do me no harm if I eat it?'

'No,' said the Woman, braiding up her hair, 'eat it quickly and I will ever be grateful to you.'

Cat made one jump and caught the little mouse, and the Woman said, 'A hundred thanks. Even the First Friend is not quick enough to catch little mice as you have done. You must be very wise.'

That very minute and second, O Best Beloved, the Milk-pot that stood by the fire cracked in two pieces – *ffft!* – because it remembered the bargain she had made with the Cat; and when the Woman jumped down from the footstool – lo and behold! – the Cat was lapping up the warm white milk that lay in one of the broken pieces.

'O my Enemy and Wife of my Enemy and Mother of my Enemy,' said the Cat, 'it is I: for you have spoken three words in my praise, and now I can drink the warm white milk three times a day for always and always and always. But *still* I am the Cat who walks by himself, and all places are alike to me.'

Then the Woman laughed and set the Cat a bowl of the warm white milk and said, 'O Cat, you are as clever as a man, but remember that your bargain was not made with the Man or the Dog, and I do not know what they will do when they come home.'

'What is that to me?' said the Cat. 'If I have my place in the Cave by the fire and my warm white milk three times a day I do not care what the Man or the Dog can do.'

That evening when the Man and the Dog came into the Cave, the Woman told them all the story of the bargain, while the Cat sat by the fire and smiled. Then the Man said, 'Yes, but he had not made a bargain with *me* or with all proper Men after me.' Then he took off his two leather boots and he took up his little stone axe (that makes three) and he fetched a piece of wood and a hatchet (that is five altogether), and he set them out in a row and he said, 'Now we will make *our* bargain. If you do not catch mice when you are in the Cave for always and always and always, I will throw these five things at you whenever I see you, and so shall all Men do after me.'

'Ah!' said the Woman, listening. 'This is a very clever Cat, but he is not so clever as my Man.'

The Cat counted the five things (and they looked very knobby) and he said, 'I will catch mice when I am in the Cave for always and always and always; but *still* I am the Cat who walks by himself, and all places are alike to me.'

'Not when I am near,' said the Man. 'If you had not said that last I would have put all these things away for always and always and always; but now I am going to throw my two boots and my little stone axe (that makes three) at you whenever I meet you. And so shall all proper Men do after me!'

Then the Dog said, 'Wait a minute. He has not made a bargain with *me* or with all proper Dogs after me.' And he showed his teeth and said, 'If you are not kind to the Baby while I am in the Cave for always and always and always, I will hunt you till I catch you, and when I catch you I will bite you. And so shall all proper Dogs do after me.'

'Ah!' said the Woman, listening. 'This is a very clever Cat, but he is not so clever as the Dog.'

Cat counted the Dog's teeth (and they looked very pointed) and he said, 'I will be kind to the Baby while I am in the Cave, as long as he does not pull my tail too hard, for always and always and always. But *still* I am the Cat who walks by himself, and all places are alike to me.'

'Not when I am near,' said the Dog. 'If you had not said that last I would have shut my mouth for always and always and always; but *now* I am going to hunt you up a tree whenever I meet you. And so shall all proper Dogs do after me.'

Then the Man threw his two boots and his little stone axe (that makes three) at the Cat, and the Cat ran out of the Cave and the Dog chased him up a tree; and from that day to this, Best Beloved, three proper Men out of five will always throw things at a Cat whenever they meet him, and all proper Dogs will chase him up a tree. But the Cat keeps his side of the bargain too. He will kill mice, and he will be kind to Babies when he is in the house, just as long as they do not pull his tail too hard. But when he has done that, and between times, and when the moon gets up and night comes, he is the Cat that walks by himself, and all places are alike to him. Then he goes out to the Wet Wild Woods or up the Wet Wild Trees or on the Wet Wild Roofs, waving his wild tail and walking by his wild lone.

Tom Thumb

IN A WET LAND, FLAT LAND, farther-away-than-that land lived a farmer and his wife. Every evening they would sit by the fire and talk of do's and don'ts and will's and won'ts: nothing special, but often they would laugh. Sometimes they couldn't even remember what it was they laughed at – but it was always funny. One thing they often talked about was how much work they had to do – and who was to do it?

Sometimes when they had laughed a lot and the evening drew on, they would grow sleepy; then they would become a little sad and talk of children. They had none of their own and this made them feel lonely.

"Oh, if only I had a son of my own. He could keep me company in the fields," said the farmer. "If I had but one wish, it would be for a son – even a little one," and the old man chuckled softly to himself at the thought.

"If I had a son to love and to hug then I'd not be lonely when you're out working, m'dear." The old woman warmed her hands in front of the fire. Holding one up she said: "Just as big as this thumb, he need be no bigger!" Once more they broke into a merry chuckle and rocked back in their comfy chairs.

Surely it must have been the night when wishes were granted for the following morning a very strange thing happened. The farmer had gone out to the fields and his wife was about to make some bread. She took down her great jar of flour; then some salt and a little yeast, and then a big jug of water. She started to mix and knead, knead and mix; suddenly, the pastry in her hands went "POP!"

"Hello mother!" said a cheery voice. There, on the kitchen table and covered in flour from top to toe, stood a tiny boy – no bigger than the old woman's thumb!

"Well I never!" she said and her shoulders bobbed up and down as she

chuckled at the little lad's antics. He was dancing about on the table amid a cloud of flour.

"Well I never!" said the astonished farmer when he came home for lunch.

"Hello father, can I come with you this afternoon and help in the fields?" said the tiny figure.

"Well, my little Tom Thumb, of course you can. But I've got to take out the big cart to collect up all the beet I've dug. It's very high and I doubt you're tall enough to help me load it."

"But that's no problem. I'll drive the cart while you load it with beet." And Tom clapped his tiny hands together as the matter was settled.

"All you need do," he went on, "is place me behind the horse's ear and I'll guide him along beside you."

The farmer chuckled and chortled and his good wife laughed.

That afternoon the farmer stooped and heaved the piles of fresh-dug beet into the back of the cart. Each time he moved to the next pile, a small voice called out: "Giddyup! Move along there!" The horse would prick up his ears and take a few paces more to keep up with the farmer.

Nearby, two rascals watched with open mouths. A horse that moved and pulled a cart without a driver? Whatever next!

"Giddyup! Move along there!" And again the horse moved on.

"A horse that walks and *talks*?" One rascal croaked.

"Indeed, a speciality," said the other. "I think it's worth a second look." The first rascal stepped forward right on to the toes of the second rascal and they fell in a tangled heap amid the muddy beet. Clumsily they struggled to their feet and went towards the farmer.

"Now if we smile, we'll hide our guile."

The farmer watched the two rascals draw near but stooping low he tended to his work.

"Good day, kind sir. My, what a horse! To guide itself without recourse . . . to driver or what else, heh! heh!" The rascals smirked and held their arms. The farmer winced at their false charms.

"No, 'tis just my son," was the farmer's reply, eyeing them slowly and turning to the horse that stood patiently waiting beside him. He lifted Tom down from behind the horse's ear. "He may be small but he is help enough to me."

"Well, I'll be . . ." The rascal nearest fell back against his fellow and, lying on his back in the mud, became the rascal furthest.

The other spoke: "I see," his voice was low and wheedling, "and may I

ask what price he'd fetch? I see a trade with such as he, and useful too, alongside me." He smiled craftily at the farmer. "What'll it be, my fine fellow, gold or gilders? They're both yellow!" A croaky chuckle gurgled from the villain's throat.

"Tom's not for sale. He's my own flesh and blood. I'll not sell my son, nor take your gold!" The farmer took a step backwards and folded his arms across his chest. Meanwhile, Tom had crept up to his father's shoulder and he whispered in his ear behind a cupped hand: "Go on, father, let them make you rich. Take their gold; I'll soon be back, you'll see."

The farmer nodded slowly and the gold changed hands.

Now Tom astride the villain's hat wobbled along above their chat.

"He'll make our fortune, you'll see. We'll sneak him in to turn the key."

"Then rich mens' gold and jewels we'll take. Enough for life . . . a tidy stake."

All the while Tom listened but then the two of them sniggered and tripped and down they went again into the mud. Tom flew off the rascal's hat and landed nimbly on a tuft of grass. "What now, my lords, are we to tumble all day long? Or is there work for me to do?"

The rascals leered and both bent close.

"It's very simple Tom, m'lad. I seem to have mislaid my key. That's where you come in, d'you see?"

"Yes, quiet like, and let us in. Don't wake no one, don't make a din."

Tom nodded his head pleasantly but saw through the villains' scheme. They meant to rob and steal; and to use him to help them do it. Tom was thoughtful but inside his head his brain was buzzing – he made a plan to foil their ruse.

That night the two rascals crept up to the squire's house – he was the richest man for miles about. Carefully they set Tom on the windowsill and bade him crawl through between the bars to open the door. Tom clambered through and slipped down to the floor within. Then, when he had straightened himself up he turned back to the window and shouted as loud as he could: "I'll not be long, just you wait there!"

"Ssh . . . not so loud!" hissed the villains from the window and they jostled against each other in their efforts to squeeze closer to the bars.

"What's that you say?" yelled Tom. "I can't quite hear you!" His

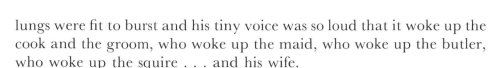

lungs were fit to burst and his tiny voice was so loud that it woke up the cook and the groom, who woke up the maid, who woke up the butler, who woke up the squire . . . and his wife.

"Stay by the window while I open the door!" shrieked Tom even louder. Suddenly the door opened, but it wasn't Tom who appeared.

"There by the window! See! Where? Over there!" First came the cook with a rolling-pin; next came the maid with a broom; then came the butler with a pained expression; then came the groom with a sharpened stick – and last came the squire . . . and his wife.

The two villains were so surprised that they took off across the fields like frightened rabbits, tumbling and stumbling over one another in their haste to escape.

Later, when the rascals were safely behind bars in the local jail, and the house was quiet again, Tom came out of his hiding place. He had been laughing so much he feared he'd be discovered, but no one had bothered to look inside the coffee-pot! He left the house and ran into the moonlit yard, seeing a large barn he entered it and lay down on a pile of warm straw to sleep away the rest of the night.

Alas for Tom, before he woke, the grumbly groom came to the barn to feed the cows and scooped up the straw wherein lay Tom. It wasn't until Tom stretched himself awake that he found he was already inside a cow's mouth. The large brown cow munched and munched and Tom was about to be swallowed!

"Oh my! What have I got myself into!" Tom exclaimed as he tumbled down into the cow's stomach. A great deal of straw was tumbling in after him and soon Tom felt quite squeezed inside the cow.

"No more, no more, there's no more room!" he cried. But unknown to Tom, the milkmaid had just begun to milk the cow he was in. The sound of Tom's voice was too much for her and she fell off her three-legged stool and upset her pail of milk.

"No more, no more, there's no more room in here!"

There it was again. The milkmaid screamed and ran to tell the squire.

"Nonsense, my dear. Cows do not talk," he said sternly.

"But sir, please sir, beg your pardon sir, it's not only talking, it's shouting at me!"

The squire decided to see for himself; so along went his wife, the butler and the cook, the groom and the maid – into the barn. They stopped and stared: there stood the docile warm-eyed cow contentedly chewing away.

"No more straw, I tell you! I'm getting squashed in here!"

"I don't believe it," said the squire and neither did his wife.

"'Tis true then," said the cook, and the parlour maid said "Yes!"

"Tut, tut," said the butler and looked the other way.

"Best to 'ave 'er butchered," said the bad-tempered groom. But the cow nuzzled into a fresh pile of straw and went on munching.

"She must be sick," said the squire. "Quite right," agreed his wife.

"Send for the farmer who lives across the field," and the groom trudged out as the squire had declared.

Within an hour the farmer who, would you believe, was Tom's father, arrived at the barn. He looked at the cow and listened to the tiny voice calling from inside it. He cocked his head to one side and then gave it a thoughtful scratch. "Well now, my lord, 'tis not much to fret about. I'll soon have her right." Then, chuckling quietly to himself, he added in a whisper: "My word, whatever will my Tom get into next?"

He sent for a bucket of warm water and took from his pocket an assortment of tiny bottles. One by one he emptied their contents into the bucket – first green liquid, and then red liquid, then blue liquid and finally orange liquid. The mixture was stirred.

At last, after a lot of stirring, the farmer reached for a large spoon.

Filling it from the bucket he whispered in the cow's ear and emptied the mixture down the beast's throat.

A few moments passed and the whole gathering drew close about the cow. The cow stopped chewing and stood very still. A strange faraway look came into her eye and a faint rumbling sound came from deep within her belly. It was clear that the mixture was beginning to have an effect and the ladies were ushered out of the barn. It was not a moment too soon either. Hardly had they left when the cow lifted its tail high in the air, gave a long low moan and "Splat!" There was Tom sitting on the floor of the barn in a most ungracious state!

The farmer shovelled Tom into a bucket while all about held their noses. Then he loaded the bucket on to the back of his cart and drove home, taking the cart right up to the pump in his back yard.

"My word!" chuckled Tom's mother. "You are in a terrible mess, my lad." She pushed Tom under the streaming pump while his father chugged the long handle up and down. She took off Tom's smelly clothes and dumped him in a bathful of suds. She scrubbed and scrubbed until her little lad was pink all over and as clean as ever he had been.

"There now, my lad, that's better," she said and wrapped him in a large white towel before the fire to dry.

"You have had a fine old day," said his father kindly. "And did you find your adventures exciting, Tom?"

"Yes father," said Tom quietly. "I've been out to see the world, but I must say it's easy to get into trouble, isn't it?"

The farmer looked fondly at his tiny son . . . "Such a little adventurer," he thought. "It's as well I've got a way with cows, Tom."

The Mice Meeting

ONCE upon a time a number of mice called a meeting to decide upon the best means of ridding themselves of a cat that had killed many of their relations.

Various plans were discussed and rejected, until at last a young mouse proposed that a bell should be hung round the tyrant's neck in future, so that they would have plenty of warning of her movements and therefore time to escape.

The suggestion was received joyfully by nearly all, but an old mouse, who had sat silently listening to the talk for some time, got up and said: 'While I consider the plan to be a very clever one, and feel sure that it would prove to be quite successful if carried out, I should like to know which brave mouse is going to put a bell on the cat?'

It is easier to make a suggestion than to carry it out.

The Tortoise & the Eagle

A LONG while ago a tortoise sat on the dusty land and watched the birds wheeling and circling in the air over his head. He grew dissatisfied with his lowly life when he saw so many of them enjoying themselves in the clear blue sky; he longed to join them and share their freedom.

'If only I could get myself up into the air I'm sure I could soar and swoop with the best of them,' he thought.

He pondered on this problem for a long time: the sun burned down and he got hotter and hotter and more discontented as he enviously watched the birds.

Suddenly an eagle came to rest on a rock close beside him and, seizing such a favourable opportunity, the tortoise offered all the treasures of the sea if only the monarch of the air would teach him to fly.

The eagle at first declined the task, for he considered it not only absurd but impossible, but, being further pressed by the entreaties and promises of the tortoise, he finally agreed to try.

Taking him up to a great height in the air, the eagle loosed his hold, bidding the stupid tortoise to fly if he could.

Before the misguided creature could express a word of thanks he fell upon a huge rock and was dashed to pieces.

DAVID FRANKLAND.

The over-ambitious often destroy themselves.

The Tinder Box

'ONE, TWO, THREE, FOUR! Left, . . . right! Tramp, tramp! One, two, three, four!'

'Good morning, handsome soldier,' said a voice suddenly.

The solider stopped abruptly. He was marching home from the wars and was absent-mindedly counting his footsteps and listening to the chink of his buckles and belts.

The voice came from an old witch sitting at the side of the road. Her lower lip hung way down below her long crooked nose and the soldier thought her extremely ugly.

'What a fine soldier you are,' she said. 'And what a bright sword and tidy pack you have. How would you like all the money you can carry?'

The soldier gulped. 'Thank you very much, old lady,' he stammered. 'But what must I do for such wealth?'

The old witch stood up and her old bones creaked. She raised a bony finger and pointed to a nearby tree. 'That tree is hollow; if you climb to the top and crawl into the hole, you can slide down inside it.'

'But what for?' asked the soldier. 'And how will I get out?'

'For the money, of course,' cackled the old crone and her long lip quivered. 'I will tie a rope about your waist and pull you up when the time is right.' The old witch drew close beside him and wagged her finger under his nose. 'Now,' she croaked, 'listen carefully. When you reach the bottom you will find yourself in a passageway lit by a hundred lamps: there you will see three doors. They lead into three chambers, each is locked, but you will be able to open them by turning the iron keys which are in place. Inside the first chamber you will see a chest and on the chest you will see a dog with eyes the size of teacups.'

The soldier gulped again and looked a little worried.

'Don't worry about him, my lad,' went on the witch, seeing his concern. 'Here, take this blue check apron; if you place it on the floor in

front of the chest and lift the dog down on to it, then he will not harm you. Then you can help yourself to the coins in the chest. They will be copper, but if it's silver you prefer you must go into the next chamber. There, on a second chest you will see a dog with eyes the size of millstones. Place him on the apron and the silver will be yours for the taking. If silver is not to your liking and gold is your fancy, then you must enter the third chamber. There, on yet another chest will be another dog, but this one has eyes the size of the Round Tower of Copenhagen. Once again, all you need do is place him on my apron and he will not harm you. The gold will then be yours.'

'Well,' said the soldier, scratching his head. 'That all sounds very reasonable to me.' He paused and looked sideways at the old witch. 'I daresay, though, that when I come out you will want a share of the money?' He raised his eyebrows quizzically.

'No,' replied the witch hastily. 'I want nothing of the gold, the silver or the copper. Just bring me the tinder box my grandmother left there when she last went into the tree – that is all I want from you.'

'All right then, old lady,' said the soldier. 'Let's have your apron and the rope and I'll be about me duties.' He tied the rope tightly round his middle and sprang up into the tree.

When he reached the top he climbed into the hollow and slid down and down until at last he dropped with a bump into a long passageway. Just as the witch had said, it was lit by a hundred lamps, and in front of him were three doors.

He opened the first door. There sat the dog with eyes the size of teacups and it was staring straight at him. 'Golly,' said the soldier and lifting down the dog on to the witch's apron he opened the chest. Inside, the copper coins gleamed brightly and he quickly filled his pockets to the brim, stuffing coins in until the pockets bulged.

Next, he opened the second door. 'Well, I'll be blessed!' he exclaimed: there sat the dog with eyes the size of millstones. 'You shouldn't stare,' said the soldier. 'It will make your eyes sore and besides, it's rude.' He picked the dog up, placed him on the apron and opened the chest. When he saw the shining silver coins he emptied his pockets and let the copper fall to the ground. He refilled them with silver, stuffing the coins in as tight as they would go; for good measure he filled his pack as well: it was so full he couldn't do up the buckles.

Then he went into the third room. There sat the dog with eyes the size of the Round Tower of Copenhagen. The soldier was astonished and a little bit afraid. For a brief moment he stood there rooted to the spot, but plucking up his courage, he saluted and said politely: 'Good morning.' The dog's eyes swivelled round like cartwheels as the soldier struggled to lift him on to the apron. He opened the final chest and it was filled to the brim with gold coins. There was more gold than he had ever seen in his life. Quickly, he replaced the silver coins with gold and stuffed them into his pockets, his pack, his hat, his socks and his boots and every other nook and cranny about his uniform; he even squeezed coins into his buttonholes. He replaced the dog on top of the chest and called up to the old witch: 'You can pull me up now, old girl.'

Her voice echoed back down the hollow tree, 'Have you got the tinder box?'

'Oh, sorry, I nearly forgot,' and the soldier went back for it, his boots clinking as he walked. The witch heaved and pulled and at last the soldier stood back on the road. Gold coins peeped out from his bulging pockets, from the top of his pack, from his boots and his hat – he felt very pleased with himself.

'Give me the tinder box,' said the witch. Her tone was harsh and the soldier drew back.

'Why do you want it?' he asked, holding it close to his tunic. The witch made a clutching grab towards him. 'It's none of your business,' she snapped.

The soldier was beginning to get angry. 'Tell me what you want it for, or I'll draw my sword and cut off your head.'

'No, I won't,' she screamed and curled her nails as if to tear out his eyes. The soldier drew his sword and with one stroke, cut off her head. Then, with the dead witch at his feet, he placed all the gold in the middle of her apron, tied the corners together into a fat bundle, and with the tinder box tucked in his breast pocket, set off for the nearby town.

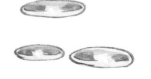

When he reached the town he went to the finest inn and asked for the best rooms in the house. Then he ordered an enormous meal of all his favourite dishes. He had so much gold that he was rich enough to buy anything he wanted.

The very next day the soldier sent out for a new pair of boots and some fine clothes more suited to his new-found wealth. He stood in front of his mirror: 'My word, what a fine gentleman I am.'

The people of the town came to make his acquaintance. They told him all about their city, and of the king and queen, and of their lovely daughter, the princess.

'I would dearly like to meet her, she sounds so beautiful,' said the soldier 'Is it possible to catch a glimpse of her in the castle grounds?'

'Oh no, that is impossible,' replied the townsfolk. 'Only her parents, the king and queen, are permitted to see her. They have shut her up in a great castle with high walls and many guards. It is foretold that she will marry a common soldier and the king lives in dread of the prophesy coming true.'

'Well, it's a pity, such beauty . . .' murmured the soldier, reflectively, but he saw that it was unlikely he would ever see her.

The soldier lived comfortably. He had many friends and rode in a fine carriage. Although he enjoyed living like a lord, he never forgot what it was like to be down-and-out, and so he gave much of his money to the poor. Because of his generous nature it was not long before all his money was gone. His fine friends stopped coming to see him; he gave up his splendid rooms and was forced to move into a draughty attic at the top of the inn.

'Too many stairs to climb,' grumbled his one-time friends and they turned up their noses as he passed.

He no longer had servants to polish his boots and wait on him; he had hardly any food to eat, and at night, when the cold wind blew through the rooftop, he would sit shivering in the dark because he could not even afford to buy the smallest lamp. One such night he remembered that he had seen a stub of candle lying in the bottom of the tinder box. It would brighten his room, he thought, and straightaway he took up the box, removed the candle and struck at the flint. As the tiny spark flew from the flint the door burst open and in bounded the dog with eyes the size of teacups. His glowing eyes lit up the room.

'Master, what is it you wish?' asked the dog.

The soldier was astonished. 'Why,' he stammered 'that is surely a

very special tinder box, indeed!' After a moment he recovered from his surprise and said: 'Good dog, you can bring me some money for a start.' The dog ran out and in a flash was back with a bag of copper coins in his mouth; he laid them on the floor in front of his master.

'Aha, so that's it,' said the soldier. It was now clear to him why the witch had so wanted the tinder box for herself. One strike on the flint brought the dog with eyes the size of teacups; two strikes brought the dog with eyes the size of millstones and three strikes brought the dog with eyes the size of the Round Tower of Copenhagen.

The soldier returned to his fine chambers and once again wore his expensive clothes. His old friends suddenly found him acceptable again. 'What a fine fellow he is,' they said, and they constantly fluttered around him.

The soldier, however, grew sad at times. He could not drive the princess from his thoughts. 'If she is so beautiful, then why is she locked away? It is such a pity. How dearly would I like to see such beauty.' This thought had hardly crossed his mind when it was replaced with another: 'The tinder box!'

He reached out for the flint and struck it; immediately the dog with eyes the size of teacups was at his side. 'I'm sorry to call you so late,' said the soldier. 'I would like to see the princess. Can you bring her to me?'

The dog grunted and was gone and back in the blink of an eye. There, fast asleep on his back, lay the beautiful princess. She looked so soft and lovely as she slumbered that the soldier could not resist gently kissing her. Then, with a sigh, he sent the dog away to return her to the castle.

The following morning, when the princess was at breakfast with the king and queen, she spoke of having a strange dream. In her dream a dog had carried her away on his back and a soldier had kissed her.

'Really, whatever next,' snorted the queen, but she gave the king a sharp look and he, in turn, was looking very worried. That night a guard was posted outside the princess's door. 'One can't be too careful,' said the queen. 'It may only have been a dream, but just in case . . .'

The soldier again sent for the princess, but although the whole town was asleep, the watchful guard was not. He followed the dog as it padded through the dark streets until he saw it enter the inn where the soldier lived. The crafty guard took a piece of chalk and drew a cross on the door of the inn: in the morning he would tell the king what had happened and, because of the cross, they would easily find the house again. The guard smirked and thought of his reward.

Much later when the dog returned from the castle, he noticed the white cross gleaming in the moonlight. He guessed what had occurred and being a very clever dog, he took up another piece of chalk and drew a cross on every door in the town. Now, should anyone try to find his master, it would be very difficult.

The next morning the king and queen, feeling very smug, set off with the guard and a host of servants to find the house marked with a cross. Hardly had they left the palace when the king exclaimed: 'Aha! I've found it!'

'No dear,' said the queen, looking a little pained. 'Don't be silly. You have made a mistake. It is here.'

'No, Your Majesty, it is here,' said the guard.

'And here!'

'And here's another.'

Wherever they looked they saw white crosses chalked on every door. The queen was very angry: she had been outwitted. Her eyes grew narrow and she thought very hard, wondering how to get her own back. At length she took up a square of fine silk and sewed it neatly into a small bag. This she filled with fine barley grain and then she tied it around the waist of the princess with a silken ribbon. While the princess was not looking the queen deftly took a pair of scissors and cut a tiny hole in the

bottom corner of the bag. It was just large enough for the tiny grains to fall, one at a time, to the ground. Should the princess again leave the castle, the grains would leave a trail and show the way she went.

That night the soldier again sent the dog for the princess. By now he loved her so deeply that his only thought was to make her his wife. If only he were a prince and not a common soldier it would be so easy. Alas, the dog did not notice the barley grains falling from the silken bag – in the morning the trail was clearly followed, the soldier was arrested and thrown into prison.

The unfortunate soldier slumped in his gloomy cell: he was to be hanged the very next day. In the confusion of his arrest he had forgotten to pick up the tinder box. Only that could save him now. How was he to get it?

At daybreak the soldier heard the far-off hammering as the carpenters built a gallows outside the city walls. He could hear the beat of drums and the tramp, tramp, tramp of the royal guards marching up and down. The time for the hanging was drawing close and people were scurrying all about the town getting ready to watch his execution. Suddenly, a boy ran past the window of his cell and lost one of his shoes. As he bent to pick it up the soldier called to him through the bars.

'Not so fast, my lad,' he said urgently. 'I'll give you five copper coins if you run to my house and fetch the tinder box you'll find there. But, you must run as fast as you can and waste no time at all.'

The lad blinked and was off in a flash and back again before the soldier had counted to twenty. 'That was quick,' he said, taking the tinder box and he handed the boy five copper coins through the prison bars. The boy ran off well-pleased with his reward.

It was time for the execution. The soldier was taken from the town and led up the steps of the gallows. In front of him sat the king and queen. The queen looked especially pleased with herself and smirked and nodded to the assembled crowd. At either side sat the royal judges and the council and the nobles of the court. Everybody waited.

The noose was placed around his neck but just as the hangman drew it tight the soldier raised his hand. 'Wait!' he cried, stepping forward. Addressing the king he said that there was a tradition which allowed a condemned man a last request. May he, he asked, have the pleasure of one last pipe of tobacco.

The queen snorted indignantly but the king could not refuse.

The soldier took the tinder box from his pocket and struck it: once, twice, three times! In a flash the three great dogs appeared before him. One with eyes the size of teacups, one with eyes the size of millstones and one with eyes the size of the Round Tower of Copenhagen.

'Help me,' cried the soldier. 'I am to be hanged and I am innocent of any crime. I do not want to die!'

A low growl rose from the throats of the three dogs and they sprang into action. They bounded towards the judge and the council, picked them up in their snarling jaws and hurled them so high into the air that when they hit the ground their bodies broke into tiny pieces.

'Oh no, not me, I'm the king. You can't do that to me,' whined the

king. But his protests were in vain and he fled in terror.
He was chased by the largest dog, with eyes the size of
the Round Tower of Copenhagen. He snatched up the king and queen
together and hurled them even higher into the air. The royal guards
were so afraid that they ran away in all directions.

Suddenly the crowd began to chant: 'Soldier! Soldier! Be our king!
Marry the fair princess! Soldier be our king!'

He stepped down from the scaffold and was lifted high on to the
shoulders of the crowd. They carried him to the royal carriage and they
rode into the town. The great dogs barked and bounded about and
everybody cheered and whistled.

The beautiful princess came to the gates of the castle and the soldier
took her in his arms. They were married without further delay and the
wedding feast lasted for a whole week. Everyone had plenty to eat
especially the three great dogs. They rolled their great eyes and kept a
careful watch over their master and his beautiful new bride.

The Elephant's Child

IN THE HIGH AND FAR-OFF TIMES the Elephant, O Best Beloved, had no trunk. He had only a blackish, bulgy nose, as big as a boot, that he could wriggle about from side to side; but he couldn't pick up things with it. But there was one Elephant – a new Elephant – an Elephant's Child – who was full of 'satiable curtiosity, and that means he asked ever so many questions. *And* he lived in Africa, and he filled all Africa with his 'satiable curtiosities. He asked his tall aunt, the Ostrich, why her tail-feathers grew just so, and his tall aunt the Ostrich spanked him with her hard, hard claw. He asked his tall uncle, the Giraffe, what made his skin spotty, and his tall uncle, the Giraffe, spanked him with his hard, hard hoof. And still he was full of 'satiable curtiosity! He asked his broad aunt, the Hippopotamus, why her eyes were red, and his broad aunt, the Hippopotamus, spanked him with her broad, broad hoof; and he asked his hairy uncle, the Baboon, why melons tasted just so, and his hairy uncle, the Baboon, spanked him with his hairy, hairy paw. And *still* he was full of 'satiable curtiosity! He asked questions about everything that he saw, or heard, or felt, or smelt, or touched, and all his uncles and his aunts spanked him. And still he was full of 'satiable curtiosity!

One fine morning in the middle of the Precession of the Equinoxes this 'satiable Elephant's Child asked a new fine question that he had never asked before. He asked, 'What does the Crocodile have for dinner?' Then everybody said, 'Hush!' in a loud and dretful tone, and they spanked him immediately and directly, without stopping, for a long time.

By and by, when that was finished, he came upon Kolokolo Bird sitting in the middle of a wait-a-bit thorn-bush, and he said, 'My father has spanked me, and my mother has spanked me; all my aunts and uncles have spanked me for my 'satiable curtiosity; and *still* I want to know what the Crocodile has for dinner!'

Then Kolokolo Bird said, with a mournful cry, 'Go to the banks of the great grey-green, greasy Limpopo River, all set about with fever-trees, and find out.'

He asked the Giraffe, what made his skin spotty

That very next morning, when there was nothing left of the Equinoxes, because the Precession had preceded according to precedent, this 'satiable Elephant's Child took a hundred pounds of bananas (the little short red kind), and a hundred pounds of sugar-cane (the long purple kind), and seventeen melons (the greeny-crackly kind), and said to all his dear families, 'Good-bye. I am going to the great grey-green, greasy Limpopo River, all set about with fever-trees, to find out what the Crocodile has for dinner.' And they all spanked him once more for luck, though he asked them most politely to stop.

Then he went away, a little warm, but not at all astonished, eating melons, and throwing the rind about, because he could not pick it up.

He went from Graham's Town to Kimberley, and from Kimberley to Khama's Country, and from Khama's Country he went east by north, eating melons all the time, till at last he came to the banks of the great grey-green, greasy Limpopo River, all set about with fever-trees, precisely as Kolokolo Bird had said.

Now you must know and understand, O Best Beloved, that till that very week, and day, and hour, and minute, this 'satiable Elephant's Child had never seen a Crocodile, and did not know what one was like. It was all his 'satiable curtiosity.

The first thing that he found was a Bi-Coloured-Python-Rock-Snake curled round a rock.

''Scuse me,' said the Elephant's Child most politely, 'but have you seen such a thing as a Crocodile in these promiscuous parts?'

'*Have* I seen a Crocodile?' said the Bi-Coloured-Python-Rock-Snake, in a voice of dretful scorn. 'What will you ask me next?'

''Scuse me,' said the Elephant's Child, 'but could you kindly tell me what he has for dinner?'

Then the Bi-Coloured-Python-Rock-Snake uncoiled himself very quickly from the rock, and spanked the Elephant's Child with his scalesome, flailsome tail.

'That is odd,' said the Elephant's Child, 'because my father and my mother, and my uncle and my aunt, not to mention my other aunt, the Hippopotamus, and my other uncle, the Baboon, have all spanked me for my 'satiable curtiosity – and I suppose this is the same thing.'

So he said good-bye very politely to the Bi-Coloured-Python-Rock-Snake, and helped to coil him up on the rock again, and went on, a little warm, but not at all astonished, eating melons, and throwing the rind about, because he could not pick it up, till he trod on what he thought was a log of wood at the very edge of the great grey-green, greasy Limpopo River, all set about with fever-trees.

But it was really the Crocodile, O Best Beloved, and the Crocodile winked one eye – like this!

''Scuse me,' said the Elephant's Child most politely, 'but do you happen to have seen a Crocodile in these promiscuous parts?'

Then the Crocodile winked the other eye, and lifted half his tail out of the mud; and the Elephant's Child stepped back most politely, because he did not wish to be spanked again.

'Come hither, Little One,' said the Crocodile. 'Why do you ask such things?'

''Scuse me,' said the Elephant's Child most politely, 'but my father has spanked me, my mother has spanked me, not to mention my tall aunt, the Ostrich, and my tall uncle, the Giraffe, who can kick ever so hard, as well as my broad aunt, the Hippopotamus, and my hairy uncle, the Baboon, *and* including the Bi-Coloured-Python-Rock-Snake, with the scalesome, flailsome tail, just up the bank, who spanks harder than any of them; and *so*, if it's quite all the same to you, I don't want to be spanked any more.'

'Come hither, Little One,' said the Crocodile, 'for I am the Crocodile,' and he wept crocodile-tears to show it was quite true.

Then the Elephant's Child grew all breathless, and panted, and kneeled down on the bank and said, 'You are the very person I have been looking for all these long days. Will you please tell me what you have for dinner?'

'Come hither, Little one,' said the Crocodile, 'and I'll whisper.'

Then the Elephant's Child put his head down close to the Crocodile's musky, tusky mouth, and the Crocodile caught him by his little nose, which up to that very week, day, hour, and minute, had been no bigger than a boot, though much more useful.

'I think,' said the Crocodile – and he said it between his teeth, like this – 'I think to-day I will begin with Elephant's Child!'

At this, O Best Beloved, the Elephant's Child was much annoyed, and he said, speaking through his nose, like this, 'Led go! You are hurtig be!'

Then the Bi-Coloured-Python-Rock-Snake scuffled down from the bank and said, 'My young friend, if you do not now, immediately and instantly, pull as hard as ever you can, it is my opinion that your acquaintance in the large-pattern leather ulster' (and by this he meant the Crocodile) 'will jerk you into yonder limpid stream before you can say Jack Robinson.'

This is the way Bi-Coloured-Python-Rock-Snakes always talk.

Then the Elephant's Child sat back on his little haunches, and pulled, and pulled, and pulled, and his nose began to stretch. And the Crocodile floundered into the water, making it all creamy with great sweeps of his tail, and *he* pulled, and pulled, and pulled.

And the Elephant's Child's nose kept on stretching; and the Elephant's Child spread all his little four legs and pulled, and pulled, and pulled, and his nose kept on stretching; and the Crocodile threshed his tail like an oar, and *he* pulled, and pulled, and pulled, and at each pull the Elephant's Child's nose grew longer and longer – and it hurt him hijjus!

Then the Elephant's Child felt his legs slipping, and he said through his nose, which was now nearly five feet long, 'This is too butch for be!'

Then the Bi-Coloured-Python-Rock-Snake came down from the bank, and knotted himself in a double-clove-hitch round the Elephant's Child's hind-legs, and said, 'Rash and inexperienced traveller, we will now seriously devote ourselves to a little high tension, because if we do not, it is my impression that yonder self-propelling man-of-war with the armour-plated upper deck' (and by this, O Best Beloved, he meant the Crocodile) 'will permanently vitiate your future career.'

That is the way all Bi-Coloured-Python-Rock-Snakes always talk.

So he pulled, and the Elephant's Child pulled, and the Crocodile pulled; but the Elephant's Child and the Bi-Coloured-Python-Rock-Snake pulled hardest; and at last the Crocodile let go of the Elephant's

And the Crocodile threshed his tail like an oar

Child's nose with a plop that you could hear all up and down the Limpopo.

Then the Elephant's Child sat down most hard and sudden; but first he was careful to say 'Thank you' to the Bi-Coloured-Python-Rock-Snake; and next he was kind to his poor pulled nose, and wrapped it all up in cool banana leaves, and hung it in the great grey-green, greasy Limpopo to cool.

'What are you doing that for?' said the Bi-Coloured-Python-Rock-Snake.

''Scuse me,' said the Elephant's Child, 'but my nose is badly out of shape, and I am waiting for it to shrink.'

'Then you will have to wait a long time,' said the Bi-Coloured-Python-Rock-Snake. 'Some people do not know what is good for them.'

The Elephant's Child sat there for three days waiting for his nose to shrink. But it never grew any shorter, and, besides, it made him squint. For, O Best Beloved, you will see and understand that the Crocodile had pulled it out into a really truly trunk same as all Elephants have to-day.

At the end of the third day a fly came and stung him on the shoulder, and before he knew what he was doing he lifted up his trunk and hit that fly dead with the end of it.

''Vantage number one!' said the Bi-Coloured-Python-Rock-Snake. 'You couldn't have done that with a mere-smear nose. Try and eat a little now.'

Before he thought what he was doing the Elephant's Child put out his trunk and plucked a large bundle of grass, dusted it clean against his forelegs, and stuffed it into his own mouth.

''Vantage number two!' said the Bi-Coloured-Python-Rock-Snake. 'You couldn't have done that with a mere-smear nose. Don't you think the sun is very hot here?'

'It is,' said the Elephant's Child, and before he thought what he was doing he schlooped up a schloop of mud from the banks of the great grey-green, greasy Limpopo, and slapped it on his head, where it made a cool schloopy-sloshy mud-cap all trickly behind his ears.

''Vantage number three!' said the Bi-Coloured-Python-Rock-Snake. 'You couldn't have done that with a mere-smear nose. Now how do you feel about being spanked again?'

''Scuse me,' said the Elephant's Child, 'but I should not like it at all.'

'How would you like to spank somebody?' said the Bi-Coloured-Python-Rock-Snake.

'I should like it very much indeed,' said the Elephant's Child.

'Well,' said the Bi-Coloured-Python-Rock-Snake, 'you will find that new nose of yours very useful to spank people with.'

'Thank you,' said the Elephant's Child, 'I'll remember that; and now I think I'll go home to all my dear families and try.'

So the Elephant's Child went home across Africa frisking and whisking his trunk. When he wanted fruit to eat he pulled fruit down from a tree, instead of waiting for it to fall as he used to do. When he wanted grass he plucked grass up from the ground, instead of going on his knees as he used to do. When the flies bit him he broke off the branch of a tree and used it as a fly-whisk; and he made himself a new, cool, slushy-squshy mud-cap whenever the sun was hot. When he felt lonely walking through Africa he sang to himself down his trunk, and the noise was louder than several brass bands. He went specially out of his way to find a broad Hippopotamus (she was no relation of his), and he spanked her very hard, to make sure that the Bi-Coloured-Python-Rock-Snake had spoken the truth about his new trunk. The rest of the time he picked up the melon-rinds that he had

He shouted at his aunt, and blew bubbles in her ear

dropped on his way to the Limpopo – for he was a Tidy Pachyderm.

One dark evening he came back to all his dear families, and he coiled up his trunk and said, 'How do you do?' They were very glad to see him, and immediately said, 'Come here and be spanked for your 'satiable curtiosity.'

'Pooh,' said the Elephant's Child. 'I don't think you peoples know anything about spanking; but *I* do, and I'll show you.'

Then he uncurled his trunk and knocked two of his dear brothers head over heels.

'O Bananas!' said they, 'where did you learn that trick, and what have you done to your nose?'

'I got a new one from the Crocodile on the banks of the great grey-green, greasy Limpopo River,' said the Elephant's Child. 'I asked him what he had for dinner, and he gave me this to keep.'

'It looks very ugly,' said his hairy uncle, the Baboon.

'It does,' said the Elephant's Child. 'But it's very useful,' and he picked up his hairy uncle, the Baboon, by one hairy leg, and hove him into a hornets' nest.

Then that bad Elephant's Child spanked all his dear families for a long time, till they were very warm and greatly astonished. He pulled out his tall Ostrich aunt's tail-feathers; and he caught his tall uncle, the Giraffe, by the hind-leg, and dragged him through a thorn-bush; and he shouted at his broad aunt, the Hippopotamus, and blew bubbles into her ear when she was sleeping in the water after meals; but he never let any one touch Kolokolo Bird.

At last things grew so exciting that his dear families went off one by one in a hurry to the banks of the great grey-green, greasy Limpopo River, all set about with fever-trees, to borrow new noses from the Crocodile. When they came back nobody spanked anybody any more; and ever since that day, O Best Beloved, all the Elephant's you will ever see, besides all those that you won't, have trunks precisely like the trunk of the 'satiable Elephant's Child.

The Stag & the Pool

ONE summer's day a stag stepped from within a bank of willows and bent to drink from a clear spring. He lapped thirstily and then, as the ringed water grew still again, he paused and saw himself reflected in the pool.

He remained motionless for some time, surveying his shape from head to foot. His dark eyes glowed with pride as he looked at his fine head: 'Ah!' he said, 'what glorious branching antlers I have! How gracefully they adorn my fine brow, giving such an agreeable turn to my whole face! If only my entire body were so well-proportioned and beautiful then I would hide from no-one. But my legs! – I really am ashamed to see them. I know what need we stags have of them and how lost we would be without them, but for my part, I find them so very slender and unsightly that I would rather have none at all.'

The stag mused for a while when suddenly his thoughts were shattered by a distant call. Alarmed, he listened intently to the sounds of the approaching huntsmen and the hounds who had tracked his scent. Away he flew in some consternation, bounding over meadow and brush, and leaving the dogs and men a vast distance behind him.

Darting this way and that he ran on. Coming upon a thick copse he plunged, without thinking, into the gloom of the trees. However, ill-fortune struck and he became fast entangled by his horns in a twisted thicket. Tossing his head from side to side he succeeded only in further ensnaring himself. The baying of the hounds drew nearer until eventually they tore him, still struggling, from the thicket.

Knowing what was to happen to him, in the pangs of death, he lifted his head despairingly: 'Unhappy creature that I am,' he cried, 'I realize too late that my antlers, on which I had prided myself, have been the cause of my undoing – and my legs, that I so much despised, were the only thing that could have saved me.'

Usefulness is more important than beauty.

Snow White

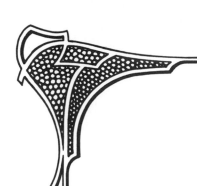T WAS THE MIDDLE OF WINTER and broad flakes of snow were tumbling and swirling around in the cold night air. Dark shadows crept into every nook and cranny and stood out sharply against the pale silver glow reflected from the moonlit snowdrifts. The small creatures of the forest had taken refuge, huddling deep in their nests far below the frozen shroud that lay across the land.

High on a hill above the ice-latticed treetops stood a castle. It rested like a great black rock amidst the gleaming whiteness that surrounded it. Its turrets and walls were dark and gloomy in the creaking chill, blind save for a solitary golden glow high up in one corner of its ebony façade. The glow came from a tiny window and it flickered like a dying star as the snowflakes danced past it.

Close by the window sat a queen quietly sewing and looking out over the frosty scene. She had a child within her whose birth was near, but despite the joy this brought her, there was a sadness in her heart. As she measured her stitches she prayed for strength, for the cold of the long winter had entered her bones and she felt frail and weak.

Suddenly, she started, as the sharp needle pierced her finger and three drops of blood fell on to the snow-covered windowsill. She gazed thoughtfully at the crimson stains colouring the white snow and her sad eyes filled with tears.

"Would that my child be a daughter with skin as white as that snow, with cheeks as rosy red as blood and hair as ebony black as the window-frame."

Outside the wind gusted wildly and the long night wore on.

The good queen died but her child was, indeed, a daughter. The queen had died that the child should live, but just before she closed her eyes for

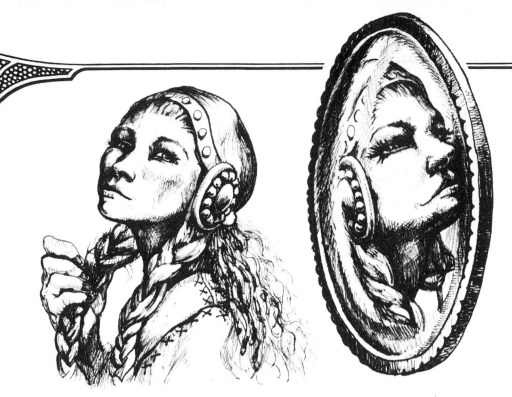

the last time she saw that her wish had come true – the child's skin was as fair as driven snow, her cheeks were rosy blood-red and her shining hair was as black as ebony. The queen's lips had trembled; "I will call her Snow White," she murmured.

The king, though saddened at his wife's death, married again and took for himself a woman of a different nature. His new queen was tall and beautiful, but her heart was cold and her pride extreme. She would spend hours attending to her appearance and scold her maidservant cruelly if her hair was not just right. She dressed in the finest robes and her vanity was such that each of her fingers was adorned with precious stones of jet and sapphire. Her arrogance was so great that she could not bear to think for a minute that anyone could surpass her in beauty or charm. Each day she gazed at her reflection in her mirror – it was a magic looking-glass and she would speak to it.

> *"Tell me, mirror, tell me true,*
> *Of all the fair maids in the land,*
> *Who is the fairest? Tell me who?"*

And the mirror would answer,

> *"Thou, queen, that before me stand,*
> *Art the fairest in the land."*

But as time went by and the years passed, Snow White grew to be more and more beautiful. By the time she was seven years old she was as bright as the morning sunshine, her ebony hair glistened about her pure rosy-cheeked face and fell around her snow-white shoulders. She was equally as beautiful as any maid throughout the land and certainly as fair as the queen herself.

The queen became cold and distant to the child and treated her with scorn. Inside her cruel heart she nurtured a hatred for the girl's sweet nature and beautiful form. At last there came a day when her worst fears were realised: as was her habit she had gone to consult her magic mirror and was astonished by its reply.

> *"Thou, queen, may fair and beauteous be,*
> *But Snow White is lovelier now than thee."*

The queen could not believe her ears and repeated her question again and again, but the mirror's answer remained the same.

> *"Thou, queen, may fair and beauteous be,*
> *But Snow White is lovelier now than thee."*

Instantly the queen flew into a rage and her frenzied anger was so fearsome that her terrified maid fled from the chamber. Seething with envy the queen sent for her groom. He stood before her nervously shuffling his feet as he listened to her cruel plan. Her fury boiled over and she paced back and forth with her eyes blazing, spitting out her words with unconcealed venom and hatred.

"You will take her from my sight!" she screamed. "Into the darkest depths of the forest . . . and there you will cut her throat! Be sure to do your work well and see that I never set eyes on her again!"

The groom hurried fearfully from the queen's evil presence lest she turn her spite on him. Straightaway he took Snow White from the castle and led her deep into the forest.

They walked for a long time and it began to get dark; the groom bade her sit down and rest. He sat a little apart from her and slumped sadly against a tree resting his head in his hands and shaking it worriedly. The weight of his duty was heavy on his conscience; during their long walk Snow White's good nature had charmed him and her soft smile had made him pity her. He told her of the queen's command, and of his fear of being punished if he should fail. Now his heart was full of sadness and he couldn't bring himself to carry out the wicked orders. He rose and came close beside her; resting his hand on her shoulder he said: "No! I will not slay thee!" He had made up his mind. "I'll take my chances with the

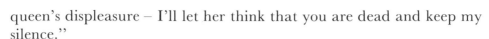

queen's displeasure – I'll let her think that you are dead and keep my silence.''

Snow White thanked him for his kindness in sparing her life and he turned and walked off quickly down the path.

Snow White was alone in the dark forest. She found a hollow beneath a great oak tree and crawled inside to try to sleep. All around her the night closed in and strange sombre shadows flitted between the thick trees. She listened to the fearful night sounds of the forest and trembled for her life – a deep throaty growl nearby, told her that wolves were about. She saw them approach and her alarm grew, but they stopped and sat close by, like silent sentinels, and did not molest her. At last, overcome by exhaustion, she fell into a troubled sleep.

She woke as something prodded against her left cheek, she opened her eyes and found a fawn nuzzling against her. The wolves had disappeared and the sun was high above the treetops. Dancing shafts of light filtered through the interwoven branches over her head and warmed her face. She smiled and reached out to pat the dappled fawn but her movement startled it and it scampered away. Birds were singing in the trees and somewhere out of sight she could hear the busy chattering of squabbling squirrels. Cheerfully she picked herself up and set off through the green sunny forest.

Late in the afternoon she began to feel hungry and looked around to see if there were any berries growing near that she might eat. Peering this way and that she suddenly saw a tiny cottage almost completely hidden by the thick bushes. Had she not been looking closely, she wouldn't have seen it at all, for it stood tucked within a shady hollow in the centre of a neatly trimmed clearing. It was surrounded on all sides by tall silvery birches and broad-girthed beech trees.

Snow White went up to the door and knocked – there was no answer so she went inside. The room she found herself in was neat and tidy and a long table had been laid for supper. Seven knifes and forks lay beside seven plates, on each of which had been placed a piece of bread. Seven glasses, each filled with wine, stood by each plate, and seven chairs were pulled up around the table, one for each of the places set. On the far side of the room were seven beds with seven neatly turned down counterpanes tucked in place.

She took a sip of wine from each of the glasses and broke a small piece of

bread from each plate. Then, her hunger and thirst satisfied, she lay down on one of the beds to sleep. She found the first bed far too small and moved to the next: this one was far too hard and so after trying all the rest she picked the one nearest to the wall in the far corner. In no time at all she was fast asleep.

Presently, while she slept, the seven masters of the cottage came in through the door. They entered one by one – seven small men with seven small caps – they were dwarfs. Each day they journeyed to the mountains to search for gold. One by one they each took a lantern from seven hooks and lit them, then they sat around the table to begin their supper.

"Wait a minute!" said the first. "Someone's been nibbling at my bread!"

"And mine too!" said the second.

"And drinking from my glass!" said the third.

"And from mine!" said the fourth.

"Who could it be?" asked the fifth.

"I can't begin to guess," said the sixth.

"I can! Look yonder, on my bed," it was the seventh dwarf who spoke.

Seven pairs of eyes swivelled towards the gloom of the far corner and saw the recumbent figure sleeping soundly. Stealthily, holding their lanterns high, they crept closer to investigate. The light from their candles revealed Snow White's peaceful slumbering face.

"Good heavens! What a beautiful child she is!"

"Ssh! Don't wake her."

"Do you think she's warm enough? We'd better cover her with a blanket."

The seven dwarfs tiptoed about, fussing with blankets and tucking her in snugly. Each was enchanted by her beauty and each was mindful not to wake her, creeping about as silently as a mouse. When at last they went to bed the seventh dwarf, whose bed Snow White had chosen, shared an hour in turn with each of his brothers.

When Snow White first awoke, she was surprised to find the seven little men sitting all around her bed, but then she saw their kind faces and concerned expressions and she was reassured. She told them her story and they shook their heads and tut-tutted at her words, murmuring disapprovingly whenever the queen was mentioned.

"There's nothing for it . . . you must stay here with us," said the first. "Should you care to cook and spin, and wash and sew for us, then we in turn will take good care of you." His six brothers thought it was a fine idea and immediately began to chatter all at the same time.

"Take care though," said the seventh, looking apprehensive and hushing his brothers. "This queen has an evil heart and she will soon discover where you are." He frowned and raised a finger to his lips: "When we are at our work, be warned! Let no one in lest you be carried away!" He wagged his finger importantly. The other six looked serious and were silent.

Now, far away the evil queen paced through her castle. The groom had told her Snow White was dead and a chill smile of triumph played about her lips. She went straight to her chamber and spoke to her magic mirror.

> *"Now, glass, I shall ask of thee,*
> *Who is the fairest? Is it me?"*

The mirror seemed for a moment to shimmer and the queen's reflection was distorted, then it replied.

> *"Thou, queen, art fairest here to see,*
> *But far away in the green wood's lea,*
> *Where seven dwarfs their home have made;*
> *There Snow White lives within the glade*
> *And she is lovelier far, than thee."*

The queen was outraged and screamed at the mirror. "You lie! You lie! It cannot be!" But in her heart she knew the mirror spoke the truth. She rushed from the room and swept down to the depths of the castle to seek out her maid. She seized the frightened girl and tore the simple robe from her back. Donning it herself the queen stormed into the castle yard; there, she rubbed mud into her face and hair to hide her beauty. Her frantic efforts were well rewarded – she had been transformed from a beautiful queen into a wretched-looking peasant woman. With her disguise complete, she set off to find Snow White in her hiding place – and when she did, she planned to destroy her.

Later the following day Snow White was busying herself in the little cottage when she heard a woman calling in a sing-song voice. "Cottons and cloth! Linen and lace! Fine wares, fine wares." The words drifted through the open window and Snow White paused in her work. At the window she saw the smiling face of a poor pedlar-woman. Truly, she looked quite wretched, but her manner seemed friendly and Snow White went to open the door.

"Good day, good woman," she said brightly. "And what do you sell today?" The woman bobbed and bowed, then she darted her grubby hand into a large wicker basket. "Why, my pretty one, laces and ribbons for a beauty such as yourself." She glanced down at Snow White's bodice as if surprised.

"My my, your laces are amiss, my dear! Let me give you a new one – fine and strong. Stand straight, my child, while I set you right."

Snow White did as she was told and the woman scuttled round behind her. Taking a silken cord from her basket the pedlar-woman busied herself with Snow White's laces. Suddenly, Snow White felt the cord slip around her throat, it tightened sharply driving the breath from her lungs. In seconds the woman had drawn the cord tight and firmly knotted it around Snow White's neck. Slowly Snow White slipped to the ground as if she were dead. The peasant woman hopped about the motionless figure, then with a last spiteful hiss at the stricken child, she vanished into the thick trees of the forest.

Some while later the dwarfs returned from their labours and found their beloved Snow White sprawled by their doorway. She appeared to be dead, but then the seventh dwarf noticed the silken cord around her throat – swiftly he drew his knife and severed it cleanly through.

The dwarfs carried her limp body into the cottage and laid her gently on her bed. They gathered round with much concern, patting and pampering; rubbing soothing oil into the vicious weal on her neck and warming her cold hands in theirs. At last she gave a deep sigh and her

eyes flickered open uncertainly. They were so relieved to see that she was still alive that a general chatter started up immediately.

"Hush now, brothers," it was the seventh dwarf. "Snow White has need of rest . . . she must sleep." Then he turned to the still shaken child and added: "From now on, no one must be allowed inside the cottage! No one! The pedlar-woman must surely have been the evil queen herself, intent to do you harm. Without question she will return when she discovers her wicked plan has failed."

Meanwhile the evil queen drew close to her castle; she paused by a tiny stream and washed away the grime of her disguise. Sweeping up to the castle gate she passed the astonished guards in her ragged clothes and went straight to her chamber to address the magic mirror. Its answer made the blood run cold in her veins.

"Where seven dwarfs their home have made,
There Snow White lives within the glade.
She still lives and breathes quite free
And is still lovelier far, than thee."

Shrieking with horror and fury at the mirror's words the queen took up a cane and struck at it again and again, but try as she might it did not shatter. Its magic was too powerful and instead of falling in splinters at her feet it merely repeated the terrible words.

The queen's anger knew no bounds, and turned within her, to a cold hatred that shrouded her heart with malice. "So! She still lives! I will devise a plan that guarantees her death. The next time I pay her a visit . . . will be the last!"

For three long days and three whole nights the queen was locked within her chamber. Every second of her time was spent pouring over her ancient books of magic and slowly she devised her wicked scheme.

When the third day had closed into darkness and the bats flitted from the creviced walls, the queen emerged from her room. No one in the world would have recognised her, so well had her magic worked. Gone was her fair skin and graceful form – in its place was a creature so misshapen as to put fear in the heart of the bravest man. Her nose and chin had become extended and stretched far beyond her sunken blubbery lips; her skin was yellow and drawn tight over her bony skull – it bristled like a hog's and was covered with ugly warts. A huge hump pressed down on her left shoulder and on the same side a withered hand, its long horny nails curling together like a bony cage, clutched at a gnarled stick. It was, however, her eyes that struck the deepest fear; they were sunk deep into their wrinkled sockets and were a deep blood-red, burning fiercely with the fires of hatred and revenge.

Down in the deepest dungeons of the castle the queen's grotesque form curled over a bubbling cauldron of vile-smelling liquid. Beside it lay the dismembered remains of its deadly contents – it was a potion so poisonous that it could kill a thousand men. At last, mixed to her satisfaction, the queen took an apple from the castle kitchen. She pierced its rosy skin with a needle and injected a measure of the evil liquid. She had taken great care to choose the most delicious-looking apple; it glistened with tempting crispness yet, beyond the tiny pin-prick, it betrayed no sign of its deadly power. The queen placed it in a basket, with others that were untainted, then she set out for the forest . . . and Snow White's cottage.

Once again, Snow White was disturbed at her work in the tiny cottage, but this time she was truly alarmed at the stranger's hideous appearance.

"What is it you want?" she asked the old woman nervously.

"Only to sell my fine fresh fruit, my dear," said the old crone. "Open your door and let me in."

Snow White remembered the dwarf's words of warning and answered quickly: "I dare not. I am bade to keep the door locked and not let anyone in."

A hollow gurgle echoed up from the old hag's throat and she shrugged her twisted shoulders awkwardly, the great hump rocking back and forth. "As you please, my pretty miss, but take this rosy apple – let it be a present from me to you." And she passed the poisoned fruit through the open window.

Snow White recoiled in horror as the withered claw stretched towards her. "No, I cannot! I dare not!" she exclaimed.

The claw rotated the apple back and forth mechanically as if to show how fresh and fine it was. "Why, you silly girl. Do you think that it is poison? Come, I'll eat the same to prove that it is sound."

The hag placed the poisoned apple on the windowsill where the sun glinted on its rosy skin. Snow White was sorely tempted to reach for the enticing fruit – it looked so fresh and inviting. She watched intently as the old woman bit deeply into another juicy apple taken from her basket. Her bloated jaws chomped noisily up and down and Snow White could no longer resist the temptation – she reached out and picked up the poisoned apple. She could smell its crisp freshness as she raised it to her lips and she took just one small bite. Instantly, her eyes flickered shut and she fell lifeless to the ground.

That night the queen spoke again to her magic mirror and it uttered the words that filled her envious heart with triumphant joy.

"Thou, queen, art fairest of them all."

The seven dwarfs found the body of Snow White when they returned from work. She was truly dead and their sorrow was immeasurable. They lifted her crumpled form and carried it tenderly to her bed. They lovingly combed her long black hair and washed her grimy brow; they touched a drop of wine to her lips, but their efforts were in vain – no sigh came from between her cherry-red lips, no heart beat within her breast.

The dwarfs were moved to tears in their grief: for seven days they sat beside her stricken form and quietly mourned her passing – not one departed from his vigil to go to the mountains; not one took bread or wine, and each day at least one was seen to shed a tear.

At length it was proposed that they should bury her – it should be within the forest where the bluebells grew at their thickest. But then they looked upon her snow-white skin and it was as pure as ever – as if she were still alive: her cheeks remained rosy red and her ebony hair cascaded over her breast and shone like a raven's wing.

The dwarfs could not bear to face a single day without a sight of her fair beauty, so between them they made a crystal coffin and lined it with silken cushions. There, they gently laid her and she rested as if asleep. On the lid they wrote her name in golden letters, and beneath it added that she was the daughter of a king.

The casket was taken to a nearby hilltop and not a single day passed without one of the faithful dwarfs sitting close beside her. The creatures of

the forest came to pay their respects and stood close by – the wolf and the fawn together, like enemies at truce, united in their grief. The birds of the air flew down and gilded the casket with fallen autumn leaves and brightly coloured feathers. An owl glided silently by and paused to mourn a while; a raven, burnished black, flapped sadly at her feet and lastly, a dove with a snow-white breast swooped and cooed a last lament.

Thus she lay for a long time – as though still sleeping and yet unchanged.

It was just so when a prince passed by one day. He noted the sun glinting from an object on the hilltop and guided his horse to its source – there he found the crystal casket and close by a dwarf was sitting quietly.

He saw Snow White upon her bed of silken cushions and his heart was filled with love for her. She was so beautiful that he couldn't take his eyes from her peaceful sleeping face. He spoke to the dwarf, asking if he might carry her away to his palace: there he would set her on a golden bier where he could gaze upon her beauty every day.

The dwarf shook his head and his brothers gathered round. "We will not part with her for all the riches of the world."

They circled the casket and folded their arms defiantly.

The prince smiled and spoke kindly to them. "Good sirs, I mean to take nothing from you – nor would I despoil her rest, but her beauty has truly captured my heart. Pray, let me then just press my lips upon her crystal counterpane."

The dwarfs mumbled among themselves and, nodding silently, stepped aside. The prince approached and bent low over the sleeping figure. His lips were on the point of kissing the chill crystal when he accidentally jogged the casket with his arm. The casket trembled and the sparkling lights that danced on its surface shivered. Inside, the tiny piece of poisoned apple fell from Snow White's lips and she opened her eyes. "Where am I?" she whispered.

Later she learned from the dwarfs what had happened since she had fallen asleep. The handsome prince asked that she be his wife and Snow White consented to his wish. Together with the dwarfs they set out for the prince's palace to make preparations for their wedding.

All the people of the land were invited to the wedding feast; the nobles and the squires and the kings and queens from the neighbouring kingdoms: among these last was the evil queen herself. She was now grown old but each day still, she asked her magic mirror the same question. Since the day she had poisoned Snow White she had received the same answer, but on the day of the wedding the mirror gave her a different reply.

> *"Your beauty once was fairest, queen,*
> *But now tis gone, for that I've seen.*
> *So go and seek out far away*
> *The fairest – Snow White weds today!"*

The queen's wrinkled face creased with frustrated anger, although she did not want to believe that Snow White was still alive after so long a time, her curiosity and envy drove her to accept the invitation to the wedding and she determined to see the girl again.

Her heart pounded as she rushed to the prince's palace in her carriage; it pounded harder as she flew up the steps and entered the great hall; and pounded still more as she pushed her way through the throng of guests gathered around the happy couple. Then, before her, stood Snow White – as fair and beautiful as ever and not looking a day older.

The pounding in the evil queen's breast felt like a wild beast tearing at her soul. She clutched wildly at her throat and tried to speak, but the pounding grew louder in her ears and a strangled cry erupted from her twisted lips. Her eyes rolled and she reached out towards Snow White, clutching at the air, but then she fell with a gasp to the floor. The pounding in her cruel heart was stilled forever and she lay dead at Snow White's feet.

But Snow White and her prince lived on for many years and were happy together in their palace. Each night they dined in the great hall and always there were nine places set at table – one for Snow White and one for the prince, and seven for her faithful friends – the seven dwarfs.

How the Leopard got his Spots

IN THE DAYS when everybody started fair, Best Beloved, the Leopard lived in a place called the High Veldt. 'Member it wasn't the Low Veldt, or the Bush Veldt, or the Sour Veldt, but the 'sclusively bare, hot, shiny High Veldt, where there was sand and sandy-coloured rock and 'sclusively tufts of sandy-yellowish grass. The Giraffe and the Zebra and the Eland and the Koodoo and the Hartebeest lived there; and they were 'sclusively sandy-yellow-brownish all over; but the Leopard, he was the 'sclusivest sandiest-yellowest-brownest of them all – a greyish-yellowish catty-shaped kind of beast, and he matched the 'sclusively yellowish-greyish-brownish colour of the High Veldt to one hair. This was very bad for the Giraffe and the Zebra and the rest of them; for he would lie down by a 'sclusively yellowish-greyish-brownish stone or clump of grass, and when the Giraffe or the Zebra or the Eland or the Koodoo or the Bush-Buck or the Bonte-Buck came by he would surprise them out of their jumpsome lives. He would indeed! And, also, there was an Ethiopian with bows and arrows (a 'sclusively greyish-brownish-yellowish man he was then), who lived on the High Veldt with the Leopard; and the two used to hunt together – the Ethiopian with his bows and arrows, and the Leopard 'sclusively with his teeth and claws – till the Giraffe and the Eland and the Koodoo and the Quagga and all the rest of them didn't know which way to jump, Best Beloved. They didn't indeed!

After a long time – things lived for ever so long in those days – they learned to avoid anything that looked like a Leopard or an Ethiopian; and bit by bit – the Giraffe began it, because his legs were the longest – they went away from the High Veldt. They scuttled for days and days and days till they came to a great forest, 'sclusively full of trees and bushes and stripy, speckly, patchy-blatchy shadows, and there they hid: and after another long time, what with standing half in the shade and half out of it, and what with the slippery-slidy shadows of the trees falling on them, the Giraffe grew blotchy, and the Zebra grew stripy, and the Eland and the Koodoo grew darker, with little wavy grey lines on their backs like bark on

The Leopard surprised them out of their jumpsome lives

a tree-trunk; and so, though you could hear them and smell them, you could very seldom see them, and then only when you knew precisely where to look. They had a beautiful time in the 'sclusively speckly-spickly shadows of the forest, while the Leopard and the Ethiopian ran about over the 'sclusively greyish-yellowish-reddish High Veldt outside, wondering where all their breakfasts and their dinners and their teas had gone. At last they were so hungry that they ate rats and beetles and rock-rabbits, the Leopard and the Ethiopian, and then they had the Big Tummy-ache, both together; and then they met Baviaan – the dog-headed, barking Baboon, who is Quite the Wisest Animal in All South Africa.

Said Leopard to Baviaan (and it was a very hot day), 'Where has all the game gone?'

And Baviaan winked. *He* knew.

Said the Ethiopian to Baviaan, 'Can you tell me the present habitat of the aboriginal Fauna?' (That meant just the same thing, but the Ethiopian always used long words. He was a grown-up)

And Baviaan winked. *He* knew.

Then said Baviaan, 'The game has gone into other spots; and my advice to you, Leopard, is to go into other spots as soon as you can.'

And the Ethiopian said, 'That is all very fine, but I wish to know whether the aboriginal Fauna has migrated.'

Then said Baviaan, 'The aboriginal Fauna has joined the aboriginal Flora because it was high time for a change; and my advice to you, Ethiopian, is to change as soon as you can.'

That puzzled the Leopard and the Ethiopian, but they set off to look for the aboriginal Flora, and presently, after ever so many days, they saw a great, high, tall forest full of tree-trunks all 'sclusively speckled and sprottled and spotted, dotted and splashed and slashed and hatched and cross-hatched with shadows. (Say that quickly aloud, and you will see how *very* shadowy the forest must have been.)

'What is this,' said the Leopard, 'that is so 'sclusively dark, and yet so full of little pieces of light?'

'I don't know,' said the Ethiopian, 'but it ought to be the aboriginal Flora. I can smell Giraffe, and I can hear Giraffe, but I can't see Giraffe.'

'That's curious,' said the Leopard. 'I suppose it is because we have just come in out of the sunshine. I can smell Zebra, and I can hear Zebra, but I can't see Zebra.'

'Wait a bit,' said the Ethiopian. 'It's a long time since we've hunted 'em. Perhaps we've forgotten what they were like.'

'Fiddle!' said the Leopard. 'I remember them perfectly on the High Veldt, especially their marrow-bones. Giraffe is about seventeen feet high,

of a 'sclusively fulvous golden-yellow from head to heel; and Zebra is about four and a half feet high, of a 'sclusively grey-fawn colour from head to heel.'

'Umm,' said the Ethiopian, looking into the speckly-spickly shadows of the aboriginal Flora-forest. 'Then they ought to show up in this dark place like ripe bananas in a smoke-house.'

But they didn't. The Leopard and the Ethiopian hunted all day; and though they could smell them and hear them, they never saw one of them.

'For goodness' sake,' said the Leopard at tea-time, 'let us wait till it gets dark. This daylight hunting is a perfect scandal.'

So they waited till dark, and then the Leopard heard something breathing sniffily in the starlight that fell all stripy through the branches, and he jumped at the noise, and it smelt like Zebra, and it felt like Zebra, and when he knocked it down it kicked like Zebra, but he couldn't see it. So he said, 'Be quiet, O you person without any form. I am going to sit on your head till morning, because there is something about you that I don't understand.'

Presently he heard a grunt and a crash and a scramble, and the Ethiopian called out, 'I've caught a thing that I can't see. It smells like Giraffe, and it kicks like Giraffe, but it hasn't any form.'

'Don't you trust it,' said the Leopard. 'Sit on its head till the morning – same as me. They haven't any form – any of 'em.'

*   *   *

So they sat down on them hard till bright morning-time, and then Leopard said, 'What have you at your end of the table, Brother?'

The Ethiopian scratched his head and said, 'It ought to be 'sclusively a rich fulvous orange-tawny from head to heel, and it ought to be Giraffe; but it is covered all over with chestnut blotches. What have you at *your* end of the table, Brother?'

And the Leopard scratched his head and said, 'It ought to be 'sclusively a delicate greyish-fawn, and it ought to be Zebra; but it is covered all over with black and purple stripes. What in the world have you been doing to yourself, Zebra? Don't you know that if you were on the High Veldt I could see you ten miles off? You haven't any form.'

'Yes,' said the Zebra, 'but this isn't the High Veldt. Can't you see?'

'I can now,' said the Leopard. 'But I couldn't all yesterday. How is it done?'

'Let us up,' said the Zebra, 'and we will show you.'

They let the Zebra and the Giraffe get up; and Zebra moved away to some little thorn-bushes where the sunlight fell all stripy, and Giraffe moved off to some tallish trees where the shadows fell all blotchy.

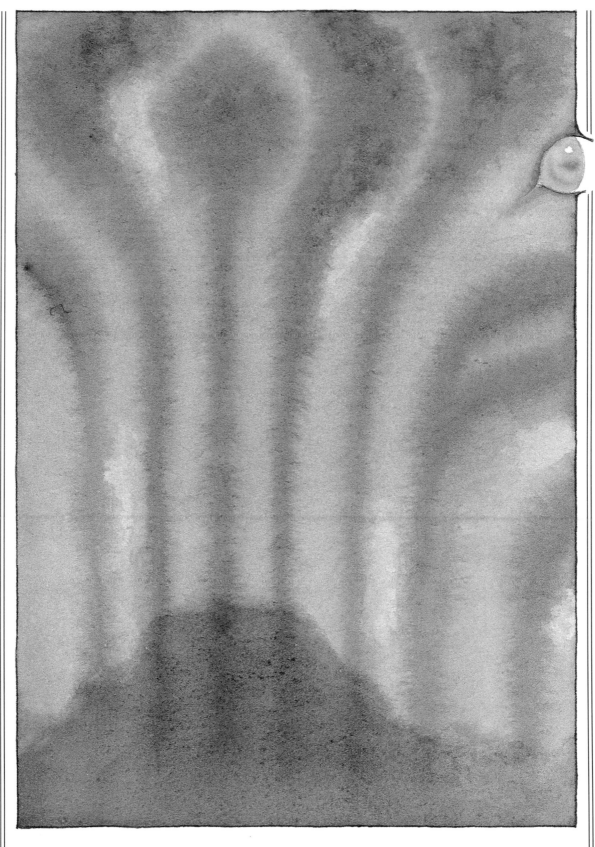

. . . it smelt like Zebra, and it felt like Zebra

'Now watch,' said the Zebra and the Giraffe. 'This is the way it's done. One – two – three! And where's your breakfast?'

Leopard stared, and Ethiopian stared, but all they could see were stripy shadows and blotched shadows in the forest, but never a sign of Zebra and Giraffe. They had just walked off and hidden themselves in the shadowy forest.

'Hi! Hi!' said the Ethiopian. 'That's a trick worth learning. Take a lesson by it, Leopard. You show up in this dark place like a bar of soap in a coal-scuttle.'

'Ho! Ho!' said the Leopard. 'Would it surprise you very much to know that you show up in this dark place like a mustard-plaster on a sack of coals?'

'Well, calling names won't catch dinner,' said the Ethiopian. 'The long and the little of it is that we don't match our backgrounds. I'm going to take Baviaan's advice. He told me I ought to change; and as I've nothing to change except my skin I'm going to change that.'

'What to?' said the Leopard, tremendously excited.

'To a nice working blackish-brownish colour, with a little purple in it, and touches of slaty-blue. It will be the very thing for hiding in hollows and behind trees.'

So he changed his skin then and there, and the Leopard was more excited than ever; he had never seen a man change his skin before.

'But what about me?' he said, when the Ethiopian had worked his last little finger into his fine new black skin.

'You take Baviaan's advice too. He told you to go into spots.'

'So I did,' said the Leopard. 'I went into other spots as fast as I could. I went into this spot with you, and a lot of good it has done me.'

'Oh,' said the Ethiopian, 'Baviaan didn't mean spots in South Africa. He meant spots on your skin.'

'What's the use of that?' said the Leopard.

'Think of Giraffe,' said the Ethiopian. 'Or if you prefer stripes, think of Zebra. They find their spots and stripes give them per-fect satisfaction.'

'Umm,' said the Leopard. 'I wouldn't look like Zebra – not for ever so.'

'Well, make up your mind,' said the Ethiopian, 'because I'd hate to go hunting without you, but I must if you insist on looking like a sunflower against a tarred fence.'

'I'll take spots, then,' said the Leopard; 'but don't make 'em too vulgar-big. I wouldn't look like Giraffe – not for ever so.'

'I'll make 'em with the tips of my fingers,' said the Ethiopian. 'There's plenty of black left on my skin still. Stand over!'

Then the Ethiopian put his five fingers close together (there was plenty

of black left on his new skin still) and pressed them all over the Leopard, and wherever the five fingers touched they left five little black marks, all close together. You can see them on any Leopard's skin you like, Best Beloved. Sometimes the fingers slipped and the marks got a little blurred; but if you look closely at any Leopard now you will see that there are always five spots – off five fat black finger-tips.

'Now you *are* a beauty!' said the Ethiopian. 'You can lie out on the bare ground and look like a heap of pebbles. You can lie out on the naked rocks and look like a piece of pudding-stone. You can lie out on a leafy branch and look like sunshine sifting through the leaves; and you can lie right across the centre of a path and look like nothing in particular. Think of that and purr!'

'But if I'm all this,' said the Leopard, 'why didn't you go spotty too?'

'Oh, plain black's best for me,' said the Ethiopian. 'Now come along and we'll see if we can't get even with Mr. One-Two-Three-Where's-your-Breakfast!'

*   *   *

So they went away and lived happily ever afterward, Best Beloved. That is all.

Oh, now and then you will hear grown-ups say, 'Can the Ethiopian change his skin or the Leopard his spots?' I don't think even grown-ups would keep on saying such a silly thing if the Leopard and the Ethiopian hadn't done it once – do you? But they will never do it again, Best Beloved. They are quite contented as they are.

The Crow & the Mussel

ONCE a hungry crow discovered a mussel lying on the seashore and tried hard to break it open with his beak so that he could get at the tasty flesh inside. He was struggling without success when a carrion-crow came along and said, 'I advise you to use a little strategy, my friend. Carry the mussel into the air as high as you can fly, then, when you let it drop down on this rock, you will find it will break open and its contents will be yours.'

The crow thanked him heartily and, thinking it a good plan, flew off, but while he was flying high on the wing the carrion-crow remained on the ground, and ate the mussel himself when it dropped down.

Some people are kind to their neighbours for their own sakes.

The Bees, the Drones & the Wasp

SOME industrious bees discovered a hollow in the trunk of an oak tree, and built a honeycomb in it. Some drones, who lazed nearby and saw a chance of getting a reward without doing any work, at once claimed that they had built it and that it was theirs.

The dispute was unresolved and so the case was brought into court for settlement. Presiding was Judge Wasp, who, being very wise and knowing the habits and character of both parties, addressed them thus:

'The plaintiffs and defendants are so alike in shape and colour that it is difficult to say which are the rightful owners. The claims and

counter-claims professed declare a difference of opinion of no small magnitude: it is therefore right and proper that this case has been brought before me.' The judge paused and crossed his wings.

'I think,' he continued, 'that justice will best be served by following a plan which I now propose. Let each party take a hive and build up a new comb, so that from the shape of the cells and the taste of honey it will be quite clear to whom the disputed comb belongs.'

The bees readily agreed to the wasp's plan, but the drones, on the other hand, would not do so.

Whereupon the wasp gave judgment: 'It is clear now who made the comb, and who cannot make it; this court has no hesitation in giving judgment in favour of the bees.'

We may know a tree by its fruit.

The Wild Swans

IN THE WINTER, when the snows come, the swallows fly away to a far off land. In that same land, and long ago, there lived a king who had eleven sons and one beautiful daughter whose name was Elise. All the king's children were very content, but alas, their happiness was not to last.

Their mother had died some years before and now the king had decided to marry again. However, he chose the hand of an evil queen who was quite unlike their own kind mother. On the day of the wedding, when the children expected to share the feast, she sneered and gave them a bowl of sand instead of food.

Her wickedness knew no limit and it was not long before she sent Elise away from the palace to live with a poor peasant woman, and not content with that, she whispered falsehoods to the king about his eleven sons. Sadly, the king believed her lies and grew cold towards them.

The queen became impatient and wanting the palace to herself, she spoke angrily to the princes. 'Go away,' she snarled, 'and look to yourselves. Fly now, fly, as birds that have no voice.' Her curse took effect and the eleven brothers became eleven pure white swans. Only during the hours of darkness could they be as men again. The stricken princes wheeled their white wings into the air and with a last eerie cry they flew from the palace.

They flew far across the wide forest until, below them, they saw the humble cottage where Elise was sleeping. They circled and swooped in the dawn sky, beating their wings and trying to peep through the tiny window of her room. But it was all in vain for no-one saw them and Elise slept on peacefully. At last, they gave up and soared high above the clouds. On they flew across the great forest until, leaving the land, they reached the waters of the ocean. Far out they flew until, just before the sunset, they dipped their wings over the horizon and disappeared.

Rose and briar grew close about the cottage where Elise lived and soft breezes played among them. 'Rose so fair,' whispered the wind. 'Who is more beautiful than you?' But the roses only trembled and answered in one word: 'Elise.' And the breeze brushed the old lady's hair as she sat with her prayer-book. 'Good prayer-book, who is as saintly as you?' And again the wind was answered: 'Elise,' said the book.

Elise missed her dear brothers, but time went by. As she grew older she became slender and beautiful; her skin was fair and her hair was long and golden. At last when she was fifteen she was summoned to the palace, but the evil queen took one look at such delicate beauty and seethed with hate and jealousy. Her cruel heart craved to turn Elise into a swan like her brothers, but her fear of the king's anger prevented her. He had given the order for Elise to be brought back and the queen did not dare go against his wishes.

However, the queen was set upon revenge and went to the palace bathroom. There, among the carpets and couches spread on the marble floor, she took three toads from her gown and kissed them, one by one.

'Go sit on the head of the fair Elise, that she may be dulled and as dim as you.

'Make your seat on her brow that her face may be shrivelled and as ugly as yours, that the king may not know her.

'Take rest on her breast that her heart becomes black and as wicked as yours, and let's not forget that she must feel pain.'

Thus did the queen instruct the three toads as she slipped them into the bath water.

The queen then sent for Elise, undressed her and helped her into the bath. At once the three toads settled on her graceful body; one on her head, one on her brow and one on her breast. Elise paid them no attention and seemed not to notice. When she rose from the water the toads had vanished: in their place floated three scarlet poppies. Her purity and innocence had overcome the queen's evil power.

When she saw that her magic had failed and that Elise was unharmed, the queen was beside herself with anger. Deceptively, she mentioned that she had some fine oil with which to beautify the skin, but instead she took a phial of evil paste and spread it on the maiden's limbs; she poured foul oil on Elise's face and rubbed it into her skin; lastly, she scooped up ashes from the hearth and mingled them in the princess's hair.

Later, when Elise was presented to the king her skin was

streaked and brown and she looked, indeed, a very shabby creature.

'This wretch is no daughter of mine!' said the king crossly and his words brought tears to Elise's eyes. In despair she looked around for her brothers but they were nowhere to be seen; then, sobbing bitterly, she ran from the palace.

She stumbled blindly along, far away and into the great forest. Her brothers must have been banished, she thought, and her heart was filled with sadness. Night fell and she had just one desire – to find them.

The sun was already high in the sky when at last she awoke to the soft chuckling of a nearby stream. Elise rose and followed the stream's ferny bank until it tinkled into a clear, sparkling pool. The bushes grew thickly to its edge, except where the forest creatures had trod a narrow path when they came to drink; here, Elise knelt by the cool water. So clear and still was it that every leaf and twig was reflected as in a mirror. She leant over and her own face peered back at her. She was astonished: her face looked coarse and grimy. She took up a handful of water and washed it over her brow, her fair skin shone through the vile brown streaks of oil. Standing, she took off her robe and stepped into the crystal water to bathe. When at last she was clean, she stepped from the pool. No princess ever looked as graceful, so fair and beautiful was she.

She cupped her hand and drank from the pool, then she dressed, braided her hair and set off through the forest.

She walked deeper and deeper into the trees until, at twilight, the shadows grew long and dark. It was cold and the trees closed about her like sombre black sentinels. A silence settled on the forest and Elise was filled with a deep loneliness. At last, exhausted, she lay down to sleep.

Elise woke early and set off. She struggled through the tangled bushes and suddenly, she came upon an old woman who was picking wild berries. She offered her humble gatherings to Elise and when the grateful princess had eaten, she asked for news of her brothers.

The old woman was thoughtful. 'No,' she said at last. 'I have not seen eleven princes, but eleven swans have I seen – and each with a golden crown, swimming in a stream.' The old woman pointed a finger: 'It is close by, I will show you if you wish?'

She took Elise by the hand and quite soon they came to the edge of a steep cliff, at its foot a spring gurgled out into a twisting stream.

'Thank you, kind lady,' said Elise and she clambered down the rocky cliff. She picked her way along the ferny banks searching for the swans, but at last the stream widened into a river and opened into the sea.

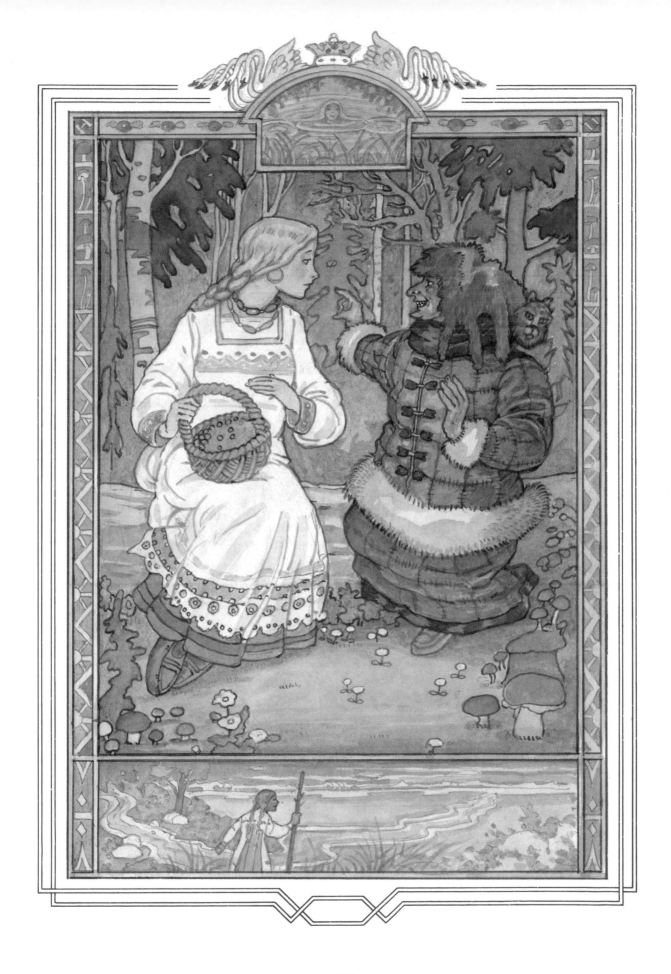

The shore was deserted: no boat, or ship, or any living being was to be seen, just the vast rolling ocean. Elise could go no further – her journey seemed to be at an end. Despairingly, she slumped down on the pebbled beach; she thought that now she would never find her lost brothers. As she sat there, idly toying with a pebble, she became thoughtful: the pebble felt smooth and round in her hand. All about her were stones and glass, iron and flint and all washed smooth by the constant waves. The waters, softer than her own fair hand, had ground down the rocky shore turning it into the fine polished pebbles beside her.

'It is a lesson you have taught me,' Elise spoke softly to the waves. 'Your waters take many years but at last shape the hardest stone. I too, must be as constant, and by not tiring, find my dear lost brothers.'

The seaweed crackled at her feet and looking down, Elise saw eleven swan-white feathers; each with a single pearl of dew – or perhaps it was a tear. She picked them up and though alone, she felt no longer lonely.

Elise gazed along the sparkling fan of the setting sun and saw eleven swans, threaded like a silken ribbon through the golden evening sky. They landed close by her on the shore and, with the sun's last radiant flare, they vanished: in their place stood eleven handsome princes. Elise had found her brothers!

She ran towards them calling their names. Their joy was overwhelming and they laughed and cried, and kissed and flung their arms about each other. The eldest of her brothers took her hand and told their tale.

'From dawn to dusk we fly as wild swans do – the sunset bids us land and gives us back our form as men. Should we be above the clouds when the sun goes down we would surely fall and be dashed to pieces on the ground.' The other brothers nodded and drew close about her.

'Far away across the ocean there is a land of great beauty and splendour and, such is our fortune, it is there that we must now live. Despite its beauty it is not our homeland and we may return here only in the middle of the year when the days are at their longest. The ocean's span is wide and the journey tiring and there is but one small rock where we may rest: no island peeps its head above the waves, no other shelter can we find. The rock is small and we must cling together closely lest we drown. If storms blow up we suffer dismally, for the wind lashes the waves into foam and whips us cruelly. But without that lonely rock we could never fly to see our dear sweet homeland.'

Elise was saddened by their story but her brother spoke again. 'We can only stay for eleven days: it is enough, but barely, to cross the forest and see our home. We can look down once more on the chapel where our dear mother lies buried. It is as if we were children again: the same wild horses gallop on the plain; the same sweet songs float up to us from charcoal-burners' camps. These memories bring us back, but sadly, for so short a time.

'Now, dear sister, we have found you, but in two more days we must return across the sea. How can we take you with us?' Elise had no answer to his question. The night wore on until, just before dawn, they lay down and slept.

Elise woke to the sound of beating wings and above her she saw eleven white swans wheeling. It was her brothers once more transformed. They turned and flew high over the tree-tops, but one sank down, her youngest brother, and stayed with her all day. He placed his head upon her lap and she stroked his snow-white wing. Later, the others returned and with the night, they were as men again.

'Tomorrow we must leave,' said the eldest brother. 'But to leave you behind us is too sad a thought to bear. As a man I could carry you lightly, so surely all our wings together could bear you up. Will you come with us, dear sister?'

'Yes, dear loves, I will be with you,' Elise smiled and took their hands.

Through the night the princes worked, weaving a quilt of willow and reeds. When morning came the princes turned into swans again: they settled round the quilt and taking it in their beaks, they flew up into the cool morning air. Elise was so tired from the night's efforts that she slept soundly on the floating quilt. Up through the clouds they flew and into the bright sunshine. The sun was strong upon her face so the youngest swan flew above to shade her.

When at last she awoke she marvelled at her magic flight, so swiftly did they travel through the air. All day the ocean rolled beneath them, but later the sky grew dark and storm clouds gathered. Her weight, though slight, had slowed them down and Elise became fearful and looked out for the lonely rock. The empty ocean spread in all directions, no rock appeared to ease her fears and she prayed to herself that her brothers' lives be spared. The sun was sinking fast and all the while their wings beat harder.

The black clouds tumbled angrily and a lashing wind howled against them. Below, the waves grew fierce and steep, and flashed from black to white-capped jade as the lightning crackled. Elise was sure they'd now all drown and she clung, trembling, to the quilt, but then the swans dived down. They plunged so swiftly that she thought the sea would swallow them, but just as the waves reached up to snatch them from the sky, the swans slowed and hovered: below them Elise could see the tiny rock. The sun fell below the broken sea in a last purple glare and as it did so they landed safely.

As men again, the brothers linked their arms around Elise, while through the night the dreadful storm raged on.

When dawn came the fury of the gale was spent but the sea still ran high and wild. Once more the swans flapped into the air, gently lifting Elise on her frail bed.

They journeyed on across the foam-whipped ocean and it was long after that Elise saw a ragged spine of mountain peaks pierce the horizon. As they drew close she saw they were thickly wooded with cedar, cypress and pine. Tiny castles and cities were dotted among the trees.

At last the swans flew down and landed. Close by was a deep cave with its walls and floor thickly carpeted with vines and creepers. When sunset came her youngest brother took her by the hand and led her to the cave. 'Here you will sleep, dear sister, and in the morning you will tell us of your dreams.'

Elise smiled at him: 'My dream will lift the curse that binds you.'

She slept and in her dreams she drifted to a high castle set among the clouds. As she looked at it a young and beautiful fairy came from the castle gate towards her.

'Is it you who will give me the secret to break the spell?' asked Elise. The fairy nodded.

'You must be brave and tireless if the spell is to be broken,' said the fairy. 'You have learnt the lesson of the soft waters on the rocky shore. But stones, unlike your soft hand, do not feel pain. They know no fear as does your pure heart. They do not suffer as you must.' The fairy bent and plucked a stinging nettle from the ground.

'Nettles like this grow around the cave in which you sleep, and others like it grow in churchyard graves: no others must you pick, only these. Let not the pain you feel deter you from your task. Scatter the nettles to the ground and crush them with your bare feet; they will burn and blister but you must not stop until you have pounded them to fibre. From the fibre you must spin thread and weave cloth, enough for eleven shirts with long sleeves. Dress each of your brothers in the shirts and the spell will be broken. But do not forget this: though it may take you years, at no time must you utter a single word. You must be silent until the work is finished. Should one word escape your lips it will drive a dagger through the hearts of your brothers. Their lives are held safe only by your silence.'

The fairy leaned forward and touched the nettle to Elise's arm. Immediately a searing pain burned like fire on her skin and she woke up – beside her lay the nettle.

Elise left the cave and did as she had been told. With each nettle she picked, her hands and wrists became burned and blistered, but despite her suffering she did not falter in her work, so determined was she to free her brothers. She trampled the nettles under her bare feet and spun the fibres into fine, nettle-green thread.

When her brothers returned in the evening they were puzzled by her

silence. Then they saw her cruelly swollen hands and one of them,
weeping, bent to kiss them; his tears washed her fingers and the painful
blisters vanished.

For a day and two nights she did not sleep and at last the first shirt was
finished. Carefully she folded it and laid it aside.

The next day as she sat spinning her thread she heard the doleful bay
of hunting hounds. She quickly gathered up her nettles and thread and
the one completed shirt and fled into the cave. Within seconds the great
dogs crashed through the bushes and, snarling savagely, trapped her in
the cave. She crouched there trembling, but then a band of huntsmen
rode into the clearing.

They dismounted and one of them approached the mouth of the
cave. He was truly handsome and was, in fact, the king in those parts.
Elise, sitting wide-eyed on her bundle of nettles, was the fairest maiden
he had ever seen.

'Why do you hide such grace as yours inside so grim a place, my
child?' His voice was kind but Elise dare not answer his question. He
bent and took her hand: 'This is no place for you,' he said. 'If your heart
is as pure as your image is beautiful, I will dress you in the finest robes
and you will live in my grandest palace.'

Elise made no protest as he lifted her on to his horse, but her heart was
full of despair and she wept bitterly as they galloped away.

When they reached the palace she remained silent. Maidservants
bathed her and wove tiny pearls into her hair. They dressed her in silken
robes and covered her ill-used hands with golden gloves. One sight of
her slender beauty as she entered the court was enough for the king; he
vowed there and then to make her his queen. The archbishop, who
stood at the king's elbow, however, was grim-faced. 'This wood-maiden
is surely a witch,' he wheezed. 'She has clouded Your Majesty's
judgement.'

The king brushed aside his protests and ordered a great celebration to begin. There was feasting, dancing and music; Elise was shown the wonders of the palace and led through its flower-filled gardens. Yet, despite the king's attentions she remained sad and not the slightest smile touched her lips. At last, in desperation, he led her up to a small chamber high in a tower. He had made it just like her cave: tapestries hung from the walls and there, on the green-cushioned floor, he had placed her bundle of nettles and thread, and the single finished shirt.

She turned and smiled at him: now she could finish her work and release her brothers from the evil spell. The king was overjoyed by her smile: she would be his bride, he thought, and he kissed her tenderly. Soon after the wedding took place.

Time passed and she said not a word to the king. Her eyes told him of the love she felt for him, but until her work was finished, she must remain silent.

At night she would leave the king's bed, go up to her little room and spin and weave until dawn. Soon, the nettle thread was all used up: only six of the shirts were finished and she must pick more nettles to complete the remaining five.

Outside the palace wall was a churchyard and in it grew the nettles that she needed. 'God will aid me,' she thought, for she was fearful of discovery. 'The pain in my hands will not match that in my heart.'

When the night was black she crept like a thief from the castle and went to the churchyard. As she tip-toed along between the graves the moon slid out from behind a cloud. She drew in her breath; not an arm's length away were the ghouls. They sat on a grave having eaten their fill, they had the heads and the breasts of women and their snake-like bodies were twisted and twined together. They watched her pass, their sunken eyes unblinking and evil. Elise said a prayer, but her heart was pounding with fear.

Later that night the archbishop sat at his darkened window, his sore sleepless eyes gazing into the night. Only he saw her step through the gates of the castle, carrying her bundle of nettles – only he was awake. 'So, I was right,' he hissed. 'She is a witch!'

Of course, he told the king and the king wept for love of his dear wife. He could no longer sleep and when Elise next left his bed, he followed. Night after night she worked in the green chamber, and night after night the king silently watched. His face became drawn and grey from lack of sleep and Elise, looking fondly at her husband, wondered at his mournful manner.

There was only one more shirt to make but she needed still more nettles. Elise shuddered at the thought of re-tracing her steps through the terrible churchyard, but that night she set off again.

The king followed her once more, but this time he was accompanied by the smug archbishop. They saw her enter the churchyard and they saw the ghouls. The king was sad beyond belief. 'How could she share my bed and lie with me, yet meet with such loathsome creatures in the night?' he wept. 'The people shall judge her,' he murmured at last.

And they did, and found her guilty – she must burn at the stake.

Elise was taken from her fine chambers and thrown into a dungeon deep in the pit of the castle. It was damp and there was no bed to lie on, but just as the jailer was closing the door, he threw in her bundle of shirts and the remaining nettles. 'Here, use this rubbish for a pillow,' he growled. 'And take your coats for a blanket, . . . not that you deserve them.' And he slammed the door shut.

Elise could have wept for joy at these unexpected gifts: there was still hope. She worked frantically all day and late in the afternoon she heard the beating of wings, it was her youngest brother. She peered through the iron grille of her window and saw him swooping by; knowing they were close gave her new strength and once more she set to work.

*   *   *

It was time! Elise was dragged from her cell and thrown into a filthy cart. Quickly she picked up the bundle of shirts and the one that was still to be finished. The crowd jeered and spat on her as she passed by, silently praying. Her lips trembled and she shivered as the cart rumbled along, and all the time her fingers sewed feverishly at the last shirt.

'See!' screamed the people. 'She is still not sorry! She persists with her wicked magic! Tear it from her! Rip it to shreds!' The crowd was angry and began to pull savagely at the sides of the cart, but a great flapping noise startled them and they drew back. Eleven swans swooped down and perched around the edge of the cart; they ruffled their feathers and hissed at the throng.

The cart trundled at last into the cobbled square; in the centre stood a tall stake and around its foot were piled bundles of dry brushwood. The people were eager to see the burning of the witch. The executioner reached up to drag her from the cart but Elise shrunk back, took up the pile of shirts and threw them over the backs of the eleven swans. Instantly, eleven handsome princes ringed the cart. Strong young men, save one, the youngest: he still had a white swan's wing instead of an arm. Despite her efforts Elise had not quite managed to finish the sleeve of the last nettle shirt.

'I am innocent!' she cried. These were her first words and the crowd were stunned into silence. Then, a whisper ran through their number: goodness had prevailed over evil and one by one, they knelt and prayed. Poor Elise, so weak from lack of food and sleep and exhausted by her labours, swooned into the arms of her eldest brother.

Supporting her gently, he told the king of their misfortune and of Elise's silent ordeal. The king smiled tenderly at his bride, his heart was full of remorse and he leant close towards her. As if by a signal the air became thick with the sweetest perfume and the king paused. The brushwood by the stake was curling and twisting, turning from lifeless kindling into a green rose briar. Pure blooms opened up their petals like a hundred tiny suns; each was perfection in its beauty.

The king reached up and plucked the highest rose. He laid it softly on Elise's breast. Slowly, she opened her eyes and looked up at him; she smiled and reaching out, gently brushed his cheek with her fingertips.

That single moment touched the whole city. And, for ever after, the king and the beautiful Elise and her eleven brothers and the people of the town were happy and contented.

The Robber Groom

HERE ONCE LIVED A MILLER who had the prettiest daughter a man could wish for. She was fair of face and form, and delightful in her manner to all who knew her.

As time went by she grew from a pretty child into a beautiful young woman. "It is time," thought the miller, "for her to marry. I shall seek for a suitable groom to welcome as a son. When I find a man I can trust I will give him my daughter's hand in marriage."

The miller gave a great deal of thought to this affair and whenever he went to the market, he would talk with his many friends and ask them of their sons. A suitable match would soon be found.

Now the miller was very rich from grinding the corn gathered from miles about. His daughter, when she married, would therefore have a rich dowry: she would be a prize for a less-than-honest man. The miller was also shrewd and although he didn't care whether his daughter's groom was rich or poor, he must on all accounts, be honest and true and love her for herself alone.

News of the miller's wealth and of his beautiful daughter spread far and wide and many would-be suitors came to visit the mill. The wily miller saw that most were merely after his daughter's dowry and sent them off with a flea in their ear.

One day the miller heard a knock at the door and when he opened it found a handsome stranger standing there. His clothes showed him to be a man of some wealth and his horse was well-harnessed with the finest tack.

The young man rested with them for the evening and talked quite charmingly of this and that, admiring the miller's house and assuring him of his reputation as the finest miller throughout the land. The miller was soon won over and encouraged the young man's attentions to his

daughter. She, as always, was politely mannered, but behind her smile she nursed a secret doubt about the stranger.

Within a week the young man asked the miller for his daughter's hand in marriage. The miller readily agreed and was delighted at having found so perfect a match for his daughter: not only did the young man possess good looks and money of his own, but by all accounts, had a fine house and estate where his daughter could live quite comfortably. Indeed, the miller thought, his motives are beyond reproach.

The miller's daughter abided by her father's wishes and consented to

the marriage, but deep within her heart she felt no love for the young man. He visited her daily and paid her compliments, yet although she measured his charm she would shudder at his touch and his silken tongue sent a creeping chill into her very bones.

One day he declared that since she was to be his wife, she should visit his house to see where she would live after the wedding. Flustered, she answered that she didn't know where his house was.

"But it's quite near," he chided. "In yonder forest, set among the tallest trees."

Still she did not visit, pretending she did not know the way.

"Tomorrow you *will* come to my house." The young man had grown quite insistent. "I will lay a trail for you to follow through the forest. I will scatter ashes along the path and you will easily find your way." The miller's daughter searched her mind for an excuse but he went on: "Besides, I have invited friends to meet you and I know they will be sorely offended if you do not come." His words got the better of her good nature and for the sake of his friends, she agreed.

When morning came her mind was troubled; something sinister about the young man's manner made her wary, even fearful. So, just before she set out, she filled her pockets with peas and beans. Then, as she traced the scattered ashes through the forest, she dropped a bean to the left and a pea to the right with every step.

It was late in the afternoon and the shadows had grown long when she came at last to a dark house hunched amidst the tall, overhanging trees. It appeared to be deserted and was cold and foreboding. The stillness of

the forest thereabouts sent a shiver down her spine as she stealthily approached. She reached the crumbling stone steps that led up to the dark sunken doorway and was about to ascend when she was startled by a shrill cry:

> *"Turn again, my bonny bride,*
> *Return to your safe home.*
> *Haste from the robber's den and hide*
> *Let it not be your tomb."*

Above her head she saw a wicker cage hanging from the portal. Inside a robin hopped about and flapped its wings. She took a further step towards the door.

> *"Turn again, my bonny bride,*
> *Return to your safe home.*
> *Haste from the robber's den and hide*
> *Let it not be your tomb."*

She smiled at the robin's antics but paid no heed to its repeated warning. She climbed the steps and entered the house; inside it was dark and gloomy and as silent as the grave. She picked her way from room to room but all were empty, there was no sign of her intended groom or of his guests. She climbed the stairs but again found all the rooms were deserted. At last, set high beneath the roof in the attic, she came upon a narrow doorway. She went in and found an old woman sitting close to a small window slanting down from the roof. She appeared to be asleep but then the girl saw that her eyes were gazing out across the treetops into the far distance.

"I beg your pardon, good lady," said the miller's daughter. "But pray

tell me if this is the house of my intended husband?"

The old woman clasped her gnarled old hands together tightly and a shadow of fear flickered across her face.

"Ah, my child, so you have fallen into his trap." Her voice was kind and she leaned forward in her chair. Her eyes widened as she spoke again: "You have come here to be the bride of Death!" Her voice was barely a whisper. "Your fine young man is a common robber. His fine clothes and horse belong to long-dead travellers. Now, he means to steal your greatest gift . . . your life!"

The old woman rose from her chair and her bones creaked and groaned. "He will return soon for his supper. I must hide you or your life is lost." She took hold of the girl's hand. "Come, be quick!"

She led the girl to a great hall and hid her behind a pile of huge wine casks. "Do not stir, my child, be as quiet as a mouse. When the robbers sleep we will escape." The old woman paused and then she added quietly: "Will you take me with you? I have long wanted to leave this wretched place, but my eyes are dim and my years bade me stay. With you to guide me I too can be free."

"Of course," said the girl and she kissed the old woman's wrinkled cheek. Outside they heard the sound of horses' hooves approaching. The old woman just had time to push the barrels close about the girl when the robbers entered the room.

From her hiding place the miller's daughter heard their rough voices and recognized among them that of her would-be husband; it was coarse and no longer carried its silken tones. She also heard the terrified cries of a young girl, made captive by the evil band. She listened to them drink and feast and heard the poor maid's pleas for mercy. She heard them force the wine to the maid's lips and heard her gasp as she fell dead.

The miller's daughter trembled for fear that they would discover her hiding place and kill her too. Her heart was beating so loudly she felt sure they would hear its pounding. She crouched lower but then a voice spoke out above the rest.

"Be still, you rogues!" It was the robber-groom. "Now that this wretch is dead, I'll have the gold from her finger." He snatched at the ring but it flew from his hands across the room. The miller's daughter heard it rolling, rolling . . . towards her hiding place. Then the ring was at her feet, tumbling still, and gleaming dully in the flickering candlelight. She snatched it up and held her breath.

"The Devil! Where's it gone?" The curse was followed by the robber's heavy steps and she heard the first rasp of a barrel being heaved to one side.

"Leave it for now!" It was the old woman's voice. "Come to your food. It's late and rabbit pie is best when hot. The ring will still be there tomorrow, it'll not run away, I'll be bound."

So the robbers gave up their search and went on with their eating and their drinking. The miller's daughter let out a long sigh and waited.

Meanwhile, the old woman had mixed a powerful sleeping draught –

when the robbers were not looking she slipped it into the jug of wine.
Soon, the robbers were snoring loudly. They sprawled across the
scattered plates and spilt wine on the long table and lay crumpled on the
floor where they had fallen in their drunken stupor.

The girl crept from behind the barrels and picked her way fearfully
towards the door. One of the robbers growled noisily in his sleep as she
passed and her heart missed a beat. In the corner of the room she saw the
crumpled figure of their murdered victim and her eyes filled with tears.

At last she was out of the dreadful room and, taking the old woman's
arm, she left the house and its murderous occupants.

The moon was high and the forest was bathed in silver light as the two
threaded their way through the trees. Rain had fallen and the ashes had
been washed away, but in their place they found the young shoots of peas
and beans sprouting up on either side of the path. They walked, all
through the night, for the old woman moved slowly, and it was dawn
when they finally reached the mill.

The miller was beside himself with rage when he heard his daughter's
tale. He sat down in his chair for a long time to calm down, and at length,
a cold thoughtful look came into his eyes.

"You may stay with us as our guest . . . as long as you wish." He told
the old woman. Then he turned to his daughter and whispered his plan.
"The wedding will take place, my dear." But she thought she detected a
chuckle in his voice as he took her in his arms.

The day of the wedding arrived. The miller invited all his friends and
relations. He had also sent word to the robber-groom to be certain to
bring his friends as well. Sure enough, the brigands rode up and sat
themselves down at the wedding table to enjoy the feast.

When all had had their fill the miller proposed that each and every
guest should tell a tale to entertain their fellows. It was soon a merry
gathering as tale followed tale, but then at last it came to the turn of the
miller's daughter.

"Come now, my dear," sneered the robber-groom. "Have you no
tongue? Do you have a tale to tell us?"

She answered lightly: "Yes, but it is but a dream I had, my dear."

The guests leaned forward to listen to her tale.

"I dreamed of a wood, and a lonely house – and a robin who spoke of
my death. I dreamed of an old woman who hid me behind a cask of wine

to save me from a robber band. She bade me be still and quiet as a mouse." The guests were open-mouthed and waited on her every word.

"I dreamed the robbers came, and with them brought a captive maid. I dreamed they forced the poison wine between her lips and I dreamed she fell dead at their feet. I dreamed a robber snatched at her finger to tear off her golden ring, and I dreamed it rolled away and settled at my feet."

A stunned silence had come upon the gathering, broken only by the sound of the robbers nervously shuffling their feet.

"And then, my child, what next did you dream?" It was the old woman who had crept from the mill and was now standing right behind the robber-groom. He was shaken by the sound of her voice that he knew so well, but he was rooted to his seat with fear.

"Then, good mother, I picked it up . . . and here it is!"

The robber looked with disbelief at the ring and his face went as white as snow; his eyes blinked wildly and he made to rise from the table. But, to his dismay, he was unable to flee: the miller had chosen his guests with care and strong arms pinned the robber to his seat. Others held his companions down and at length they were taken off to justice.

And the miller's daughter? Aye, she married a fine young man. His strong arms first caught her eye at the wedding feast. Now, she is happy with children of her own. Her husband is honest and true and works the mill. While the old miller – he sits in the sun and smiles at his grandchildren and tells them tales of long ago, of fair maidens and robbers – and clever millers.

The Old Hound

A HUNTSMAN long ago had a fine pack of hounds. He had trained them well and they were all skilled in the chase and obedient to his call. One hound, however, stood out among the pack for his exceptional ability and fearless bravery. The master had noted this, and his favour was rewarded by the hound's devotion.

This hound could outrun the stag and the hare; he could outfight the wolf and the fox; he would stand against an enraged bear and bring it down – such was his bravery. Once when his master had fallen from his horse and lay injured, the hound had remained with him all through the dark night until rescue had come – such was his loyalty.

The years passed and, alas, the hound grew old with them. Although he remained as faithful as ever, his speed and skill diminished, his limbs became stiff and his eyes grew tired.

One day, while hunting a wild boar, his master directed him into a copse. With his old legs tired and aching from the chase, the hound plunged through the bracken into the trees. There in a small clearing was the boar, snorting and angrily stamping the ground.

A ferocious battle began; the boar lunged and stabbed with his curling tusks and, although the hound fought back bravely and seized the creature by the ear, he was weakened and tired and could not retain his hold. At last, as his strength ebbed away, he released his grip and allowed the beast to escape.

At that moment his master rode into the thicket and, seeing what had happened, he severely scolded the old hound. He paid no heed to the dog's wounds and would have beaten him there and then had not the hound sadly cried, 'Please master, spare your old servant. Although my heart is willing and true, my body is old and feeble. Remember me for what I was rather than for what I am now.'

Faithful service should be long remembered.

The Kite, the Frog & the Mouse

THERE was once much argument between a frog and a mouse as to which should be master of the fen. Both were stubborn and many pitched battles resulted.

The crafty mouse, hiding under the grass, would make sudden attacks upon his enemy, often surprising him at a disadvantage.

The frog was stronger than his rival, however, and, hoping to end the dispute, challenged the mouse to single combat.

The mouse accepted the challenge, and on the appointed day the champions entered the field, each armed with the point of a bulrush. Both confident of success they charged into battle.

A kite chanced to be hovering overhead at the time, and seeing the two silly creatures so intent upon their quarrel, she swooped suddenly down, seized them in her talons, and carried them off as a fine meal for her young.

DAVID FRANKLAND.

United we stand, divided we fall.

The Little Match Girl

ONG, LONG AGO ON NEW YEAR'S EVE, it began to snow. It was the very last hour of daylight and people were scurrying about the town anxious to get home before dark and out of the dreadful cold.

As night fell, a poor little match girl trudged through the swirling snowflakes. She had no hat for her head and her feet were bare. She shivered as she struggled through the cold, dark streets and her feet became sore and frozen by the icy snow on the ground. Her hands were thrust deep into her apron pocket, clutching her bundle of matches, but the icy wind cut through the thin cloth and chilled her tiny fingers to the bone. Not one penny had she earned all day, no-one had stopped to buy her wares and not one match had she sold.

'What shall I do?' she murmured and her lip trembled at the thought of her cruel father 'He will surely beat me for not selling any matches. I cannot go home.' She shivered even more as she thought of the attic where she lived, right up under the snow-covered roof: so full of holes and cracks that the icy wind and snow screamed right into her room.

Her golden hair fell about her shoulders and sparkled like frost as the snowflakes settled on her head. She passed between the tall houses and from the lighted windows she heard laughter and caught the smell of food cooking. It was New Year's Eve and she was so hungry.

'If only I had a home so warm – and food to eat.'

At last she slumped to the ground and sheltered from the tumbling snow in a narrow alleyway. Huddled close against the wall, she tucked her feet up beneath her ragged skirt to warm them. She clenched her tiny hands around the bundle of matches. 'If only I dare light one,' she thought. 'It will warm me.' She took a match and struck it – it flared up brightly and warmed her frozen fingers like a tiny sun. She gazed into the glowing flame and it seemed to become a blazing iron stove. She

stretched out her feet towards it, but suddenly she was in darkness again, holding the burned-out match. The stove had disappeared.

She struck a second match. It burst into flame and cast a glow on the wall in front of her and it seemed that she could see right through it. Inside was a table laid for dinner: a pure white tablecloth, fine china, sparkling silverware and tall elegant glasses. In the centre of the table was a grand roast goose surrounded by baked apples and juicy prunes. As she watched the goose got up and even though it was pierced by a knife and fork, it walked towards her. Hardly had she raised her hand to greet it when the flame of the match died and her raw fingers felt the cold, hard stone of the wall.

She fumbled for a third match and struck it. This time, as it flared into life, she found herself beneath a tall Christmas tree. Her eyes opened wide as she peered up through the greenery. Lighted candles flickered on every branch and gaily-coloured dolls and toys were hung amongst them. She smiled softly, but then once more, the match went out. The candles that she'd seen were only the stars shivering above her. One of them began to fall and as she watched, it traced a thread of gold across the dark sky.

'Someone is dying,' she whispered sadly. Her dear grandmother had told her so before she died – a shooting star was a soul on its way to heaven.

Her grandmother filled her thoughts – how kind she had been and how much she had loved her. She took another match and struck it. In its light she saw her grandmother. 'Oh grandmother,' she cried and stretched her arms towards her. 'Please take me with you. I know you will surely disappear when the match burns out, just like the stove and the goose and the Christmas tree. Oh, please don't go.'

As fast as her frozen hands would allow, the little girl took all her remaining matches and struck them, one after another: so dearly did she want her grandmother to stay with her. The matches flared as bright as a summer's day and she felt her grandmother's arms around her, lifting her up and away to a place where she no longer felt cold, or hungry or afraid. The little girl closed her eyes.

*   *   *

In the first grey light of dawn the little child was found. She had frozen to death, but on her face was the lingering trace of a smile. So happy had she been with her dreams.

The wintry sun shone down on the lifeless bundle huddled in the alleyway and around her feet were scattered the burned-out matches.

The Wolf & the Dog

ONE moonlit night a solitary wolf slipped out from among the shadows. He was lean, half-starved and very hungry. As he loped along he suddenly came upon a very plump, well-fed dog. The two exchanged greetings and the wolf, looking the dog up and down, remarked: 'Sir, you do look extremely well. I don't think I've ever seen a more healthy, happy animal. Tell me, how is it that you seem to live much better than I? I may say, without false modesty, that I venture out on the hunt and put my life at risk a hundred times more often than you, yet you are well-fed while I am almost ready to perish with hunger.'

The dog grunted. 'You may live just as well as I if you choose to do what I do,' he said bluntly.

The wolf pricked up his ears. 'And what is that?' he asked.

The dog preened, as all those do with secret knowledge: 'It's very simple, I guard the house during the night and keep it safe from thieves.'

'That I would gladly do with all my heart, for at present I have a sorry time of it,' said the wolf. 'To change my life in the woods, where I suffer rain, frost and snow, for a warm roof over my head and fine food inside me, would indeed be a bargain.' The dog turned and, beckoning the wolf to follow, he set off down the road.

As they jogged along side by side the wolf happened to notice a strange crease around the dog's neck and, his curiosity getting the better of him, he asked its cause. The dog tried to shrug off the question but the wolf pressed him for an answer.

'If you must know,' said the dog at last, 'I am tied up during the day in case I let my temper loose and bite an innocent stranger – I'm only allowed to roam free at night.' He paused and then continued in a tone that seemed to imply that this was the way things should be.

'If I go nowhere during the day, then all I can do is sleep. At night,

when I am turned loose, I am therefore more vigilant. My master and all the family are very fond of me and I am fed with plates of bones and scraps from the table – my reward is considerable, I can tell you.'

The wolf stopped in his tracks.

'What is the matter with you?' asked the dog impatiently. 'Come along, don't dawdle.'

'No,' replied the wolf. 'Forgive me, but I cannot join you. My liberty is too precious to me and I would not be a king under the terms you describe.' So saying the wolf turned and headed back towards the wild woods.

Freedom is better than comfort in captivity.

The Sing-Song of Old Man Kangaroo

NOT ALWAYS WAS THE KANGAROO as now we do behold him, but a Different Animal with four short legs. He was grey and he was woolly, and his pride was inordinate: he danced on an outcrop in the middle of Australia, and he went to the Little God Nqa.

He went to Nqa at six before breakfast, saying, 'Make me different from all other animals by five this afternoon.'

Up jumped Nqa from his seat on the sand-flat and shouted, 'Go away!'

He was grey and he was woolly, and his pride was inordinate; he danced on a rock-ledge in the middle of Australia, and he went to the Middle God Nquing.

He went to Nquing at eight after breakfast, saying, 'Make me different from all other animals; make me, also, wonderfully popular by five this afternoon.'

Up jumped Nquing from his burrow in the spinifex and shouted, 'Go away!'

He was grey and he was woolly, and his pride was inordinate: he danced on a sandbank in the middle of Australia, and he went to the Big God Nqong.

He went to Nqong at ten before dinner-time, saying, 'Make me different from all other animals; make me popular and wonderfully run after by five this afternoon.'

Up jumped Nqong from his bath in the salt-pan and shouted, 'Yes, I will!'

Nqong called Dingo – Yellow-Dog Dingo – always hungry, dusty in the sunshine, and showed him Kangaroo. Nqong said, 'Dingo! Wake up, Dingo! Do you see that gentleman dancing on an ashpit? He wants to be popular and very truly run after. Dingo, make him so!'

Up jumped Dingo – Yellow-Dog Dingo – and said, 'What, *that* cat-rabbit?'

Off ran Dingo – Yellow-Dog Dingo – always hungry, grinning like a coal-scuttle, – ran after Kangaroo.

He was wild and he was woolly, and his pride was inordinate

Off went the proud Kangaroo on his four little legs like a bunny.

This, O Beloved of mine, ends the first part of the tale!

He ran through the desert; he ran through the mountains; he ran through the salt-pans; he ran through the reed-beds; he ran through the blue gums; he ran through the spinifex; he ran till his front legs ached.

He had to!

Still ran Dingo – Yellow-Dog Dingo – always hungry, grinning like a rat-trap, never getting nearer, never getting farther, – ran after Kangaroo.

He had to!

Still ran Kangaroo – Old Man Kangaroo. He ran through the ti-trees; he ran through the mulga; he ran through the long grass; he ran through the short grass; he ran through the Tropics of Capricorn and Cancer; he ran till his hind legs ached.

He had to!

Still ran Dingo – Yellow-Dog Dingo – hungrier and hungrier, grinning like a horse-collar, never getting nearer, never getting farther; and they came to the Wollgong River.

Now, there wasn't any bridge, and there wasn't any ferry-boat, and Kangaroo didn't know how to get over; so he stood on his legs and hopped.

He had to!

He hopped through the Flinders; he hopped through the Cinders; he hopped through the deserts in the middle of Australia. He hopped like a Kangaroo.

First he hopped one yard; then he hopped three yards; then he hopped five yards; his legs growing stronger; his legs growing longer. He hadn't any time for rest or refreshment, and he wanted them very much.

Still ran Dingo – Yellow-Dog Dingo – very much bewildered, very much hungry, and wondering what in the world or out of it made Old Man Kangaroo hop.

For he hopped like a cricket; like a pea in a saucepan; or a new rubber

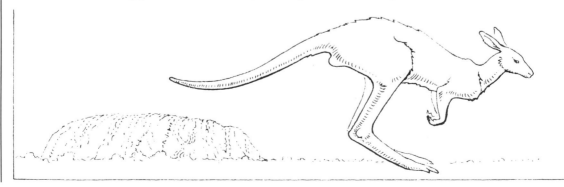

ball on a nursery floor.

He had to!

He tucked up his front legs; he hopped on his hind legs; he stuck out his tail for a balance-weight behind him; and he hopped through the Darling Downs.

He had to!

Still ran Dingo – Tired-Dog Dingo – hungrier and hungrier, very much bewildered, and wondering when in the world or out of it would Old Man Kangaroo stop.

Then came Nqong from his bath in the salt-pan, and said, 'It's five o'clock.'

Down sat Dingo – Poor-Dog Dingo – always hungry, dusty in the sunshine; hung out his tongue and howled.

Down sat Kangaroo – Old Man Kangaroo – stuck out his tail like a milking-stool behind him, and said, 'Thank goodness *that*'s finished'!

Then said Nqong, who is always a gentleman, 'Why aren't you grateful to Yellow-Dog Dingo? Why don't you thank him for all he has done for you?'

Then said Kangaroo – Tired Old Kangaroo – 'He's chased me out of the homes of my childhood; he's chased me out of my regular meal-times; he's altered my shape so I'll never get it back; and he's played Old Scratch with my legs.'

Then said Nqong, 'Perhaps I'm mistaken, but didn't you ask me to make you different from all other animals, as well as to make you very truly sought after? And now it is five o'clock.'

'Yes,' said Kangaroo. 'I wish that I hadn't. I thought you would do it by charms and incantations, but this is a practical joke.'

'Joke!' said Nqong, from his bath in the blue gums. 'Say that again and I'll whistle up Dingo and run your hind legs off.'

'No,' said the Kangaroo. 'I must apologise. Legs are legs, and you needn't alter 'em so far as I am concerned. I only meant to explain to Your Lordliness that I've had nothing to eat since morning, and I'm very empty indeed.'

'Yes,' said Dingo – Yellow-Dog Dingo – 'I am just in the same situation. I've made him different from all other animals; but what may I have for my tea?'

Then said Nqong from his bath in the salt-pan, 'Come and ask me about it to-morrow, because I'm going to wash.'

*　　　*　　　*

So they were left in the middle of Australia, Old Man Kangaroo and Yellow-Dog Dingo, and each said, 'That's *your* fault.'

Hansel and Gretel

ON THE TABLE lay one small piece of bread: it was all there was to feed three people – a poor woodsman, his wife and their son Hansel. Once, the woodman had been able to make a good living by cutting and selling logs, but now he had fallen on hard times and had no money whatsoever.

"It's no good just sitting there," snapped his wife crossly. "You'll just have to go and cut more logs. More wood to sell will mean more money to buy food! We can't go on like this, you know, we need to fill our bellies!"

On and on she nagged at her miserable husband. "And this boy of ours! He is getting bigger every day! Only seven years old? He eats enough for ten men!"

The woodsman couldn't bear to listen to his wife's ranting any longer and picking up his axe he left the cottage and went to the woods. After the noisy anger within his home, the woodsman found the silent trees around him cool and peaceful; he began to feel quite cheerful. "I will cut more wood today than ever before," he said to himself as he swung along the forest track. Presently, at his feet, he came upon what appeared to be a bundle of rags. He bent to take a closer look and the rags moved beneath his hand. Somewhat startled, he drew back in surprise, and saw that the bundle was a sleeping child.

"Why, my little love," he whispered. "What are you doing here all alone?" The woodsman brushed her golden hair from her brow and as he did so, she opened her eyes – they were the deepest blue he'd ever seen. She looked up into his kind face and told him her story.

She could remember sitting behind her father on his horse; she could remember feeling sleepy, then there had been a bump and she had found herself sitting on the forest track. She told him how she'd run off in search of her father, but it had grown dark and she had crept into a thicket and fallen asleep.

The woodsman was thoughtful: the poor child must have run off the wrong way. Her father probably searched for her but in the gloom of dusk had not seen her sleeping beside the track.

"Well now, you must come home with me," he said. "Are you hungry?" He took her hand and started back towards his home.

"Yes, I suppose I am," said the little girl brightly and she skipped along beside him and appeared none the worse for her adventure.

"It's not too far to walk, little one," said the woodsman and then he asked her name.

"My name is Gretel . . . and I'm six years old."

The woodsman laughed. "Well, you'll be a fine playmate for my young son. He's just a mite older than you, but just as bright, I'll warrant." On the way back to his cottage he caught a rabbit in one of his snares. His wife would be pleased, he thought, at least they'd have a fine supper that night, it would be a pleasant change.

Later, after they had eaten and the two children were tucked up in their beds, the woodsman's wife began to scold him again.

"Yes, a fine supper indeed! But you've cut no wood at all today and we've now an extra mouth to feed! Have you no sense?" Her words saddened him and he sunk deeper into his old chair and remained silent. He was, without question, a very poor man and his nagging wife was right – where, indeed, would he find enough food for an extra mouth?

Time passed and Hansel and Gretel grew to love each other like brother and sister but their father's misfortunes grew worse. Not only were there fewer people to buy his logs, but he had also badly chipped the blade of his axe on a fallen tree and had no money to buy a new one.

At night he tossed and turned on his bed with worry. His wife beside him hushed and grumbled and at last turned on him angrily: "Husband, do as others do! The girl was found by you so let her be found again by someone else! Take her back to the wood, and Hansel too! That way, at least, they will be fed by richer folk than us."

The woodsman was distressed and answered her quickly. "No, I cannot do that – abandon them without a care?"

"Well husband, if you do not, we will starve. You'll see!"

They argued back and forth until, in despair, the woodsman agreed to her plan – he would do as she suggested.

Meanwhile, their raised voices had woken the two children. They had heard the woman's hard words and her plan had disturbed them greatly, causing them to cling together for comfort. At length the woodsman and his wife were silent and all that could be heard was the steady snoring of the sleeping couple. It was then that Hansel tip-toed to the door and looked outside. The moon was shining brightly and the pebbles scattered about the yard gleamed like silver coins in the cold light. Hansel gathered as many as he could and filled his pockets to the brim before returning to his bed. "Don't worry, sister," he told Gretel. "I will keep us safe."

The next morning the woman tugged them roughly awake and bundled them into their clothes. "We're going to the woods today," she snapped. "Now, hurry up! I've not got time to waste on you two."

They set off, and as they walked, Hansel let the pebbles drop, one by one, along the path between the trees. Soon they stopped and the woodsman made a fire. "Stay here, my loves," his voice was sad, "while

we gather berries and search for wild mushrooms. Be sure to wait until we return." His wife snorted crossly and frowned at them without a word, then she turned her back and tramped off through the bushes behind her sorrowful husband.

The children waited and waited and listened – the sound of their parents' shuffling in the woods grew fainter and fainter. Soon all they could hear was the chirping of birds in the trees. As dusk fell, even they became silent, and Gretel began to cry. Hansel put his arm about her shoulder and threw some more twigs on the fire. "Don't cry, Gretel, we only have to wait for the moon to come out."

It wasn't long before it did, and slipping from behind a cloud it shed its silvery glow over the forest. They looked between the trees and saw the trail of pebbles, glittering like tiny stars fallen to earth.

They followed the pebbles through the night and it was close to dawn when they knocked on the door of their home. The woodsman hugged them and flung his arms about them; his heart had been heavy from the moment he'd left them in the forest and now it was filled with joy. His wife, however, smiled coldly and pretended to be pleased: inside she was secretly angry that her plan had failed.

Once again the family grew tired and weak from lack of food, and once again the woman nagged her husband. "You must take them into the forest again, but this time to the deepest part. Then they will never be able to find their way out!" Her voice was harsh in his ears. "Otherwise," she added, "we will surely starve to death!"

Once more Hansel heard his mother's cruel scheme and as before he tip-toed to the door to fetch some pebbles, but his mother had locked it and he couldn't get out.

When morning came their father gave them each a small piece of bread. He looked sternly at his wife then led the children into the forest.

"Keep hold of your piece of bread," whispered Hansel. "I will make sure we find our way home again." He crumbled the bread in his pocket and just as he had done with the pebbles, he let the crumbs fall beside the track as they walked along.

They went further into the wood than they had ever been before and when they stopped their father again lit a fire. He quickly left them and told them to wait for his return. A long time passed – they began to feel hungry and so they shared Gretel's bread.

"When the moon rises we will see the crumbs I have dropped by the path," said Hansel. "They will guide us to our home."

Alas, when the moon came up there was no sign of the breadcrumbs – the birds of the forest had picked them all up and eaten them. Try as they might, the children could not find the path leading home, and they wandered deeper and deeper into the dark forest. They ate some berries but they were not enough to fill their bellies and finally, tired and exhausted, they crept into a hollow tree to sleep.

Three days passed by as they wandered amongst the trees, but on the third morning they were woken by the sound of the sweetest singing. It came from above them and looking up, they saw a snow-white bird perched on a branch. It fluttered and sang and hopped away from them; then it turned as if to say "Follow me, follow me!" The children ran towards it but again it fluttered away only to turn and wait for them. They followed the bird until, at last, it came to rest on the roof of a strange little house set deep amongst the trees. To their amazement they saw that the house was made of gingerbread with a roof of cake and windows of sugar.

"At last we have enough to eat," cried Hansel, running forward and breaking off a piece of the roof. "Try the sweet windows, sister, they will ease your hunger, I'll warrant."

But as the children gobbled away at the little house they suddenly heard a voice call out to them from within.

"Nibble, nibble, like a mouse.
Who is nibbling at my house?"

And they answered.

> *"Just the wind that blows free,*
> *Nothing else to bother thee."*

They continued to munch away, picking at the window-panes and tearing off lumps of cake from the roof and gingerbread from the walls. All at once the door flew open and out hopped a crooked little woman with a long crooked stick clutched in her crooked old hand. Hansel and Gretel were so startled that they dropped the cake and gingerbread they were eating and stood there with their eyes wide open. The old lady chuckled and bobbed her head up and down.

"Well well, my dears, and what brings you to my house? Come in, come in! There's no need to be alarmed – I will take care of you." This last was followed by a strange deep gurgle from way down in her throat. She took hold of their hands and led them inside the house. There, she brought out more food for them to eat – sweet pancakes and nuts, apples and honey, and jugs of milk. When they had eaten their fill, she made up two little beds with clean linen and bade them climb in to sleep. Hansel and Gretel were delighted and snuggled down happily as if they were in heaven. Within minutes both were sound asleep.

However, the old woman's kindness was false, her friendly manner a deception. She was a wicked witch with awesome powers and the senses of the wild beasts of the forest. The arrival of the two children had been no surprise to her; she had sensed their approach with her keen sense of smell when they were still far away. Her sharp ears had heard every sound they made as they crept through the forest and her magic had been put to use while she waited for them. Her gingerbread house was merely a trap set to entice the hungry children. Once caught, and in her power, she planned to eat them up.

The witch hovered low over the sleeping children and cackled softly to herself. "My, how pretty they are – and what a tasty dish they'll make!" Then as the first light of dawn crept over the windowsill, she snatched Hansel up from his bed and threw him into a wicker cage behind the cottage. He began to cry but the witch shut down the barred door and locked it tightly. "There you'll stay, my little beauty, until you're fat enough to suit my taste!"

Next, she woke Gretel and shook her roughly by the shoulder. "Wake up you lazy child! Fetch some water to boil and cook up something good to eat. Your brother needs a deal of fattening before he's fit for my plate!"

Gretel was so distressed she too began to cry but it was to no avail and she was forced to do the old hag's bidding. Each day she worked and worked from morn till night, and the old witch scolded her all the time. She would cackle about and visit Hansel in his cage, asking that he poke out a finger. "Are you fat enough yet, my dear?" But her wicked eyes were dim and Hansel, seeking to deceive her, would poke out a spindly piece of bone through the bars of his cage. The witch would grunt impatiently and stomp away to wait another day.

The days stretched into weeks and finally the witch could wait no

longer. "'Tis time enough!" she hissed. "I'll cook him up with fat or not, but first I'll bake some bread to go with my meal."

In the corner of the cottage stood her great domed bread-oven and the old crone stoked it up until it glowed red hot. Then she dragged Gretel towards it and opened up the iron door.

"Here, my pretty, hop inside and tell me if it's hot enough to brown my bread."

But Gretel saw the witch's purpose and pretended not to know how to climb inside the oven. Whereupon the old witch laughed scornfully and pushed the girl aside. "It's big enough to take a horse!" she cursed. "Here, I'll show you." She bent her crooked back and poked her wrinkled head low down to the open oven door. In one swift movement Gretel seized her chance and gave the witch a mighty shove from behind. The crone pitched forward headlong into the blazing oven and Gretel slammed the iron door shut.

While the wicked witch was baked alive, Gretel ran to open the door of Hansel's cage. He was free at last and the children hugged and kissed each other joyfully. Now that the witch was dead they were no longer fearful and they went about the cottage emptying drawers and tipping up boxes and bags all over the place. To their delight they found a treasure of pearls and jewels and a great hoard of gold and silver coins. These the witch had stolen from poor unfortunate travellers who had passed her way and fallen into her trap.

Quickly, the children filled their pockets to bursting with the treasure and ran towards the cottage door. There, Gretel paused and snatched up the witch's magic wand. "I'll take this too," she said. "It will be of help, for we have far to go from this dreadful place."

Their journey took them through the forest for many days. Often they found their path was blocked by the thickest briars or great fallen trees. Gretel would wave the magic wand and the path would clear before them. At last the trees began to grow thinner and they climbed to the top of a steep ridge overlooking a wide sweeping valley. From the top, the children looked down and far in the distance saw a thin curl of smoke, winding high into the cool morning air. It came from the chimney of a tiny woodsman's cottage – it was their home!

They scrambled down the grassy slope, laughing and tumbling, and calling out happily to each other, but when they reached the bottom they discovered a deep river; it had been hidden from them by a wall of drooping willow trees. The water was dark and wide with tendrils of green weed waving gently far down in the depths. There was no way they could cross and they sat sadly on the mossy bank looking across to the other side.

Then Gretel's face broke into a happy smile – she had suddenly remembered the magic wand. "I know," she said. "I will turn you, dear brother, into a swan and you can take me safely across on your broad back." Gretel pointed the wand at Hansel and waved it around him in a wide circle – instantly he was transformed into a great snow-white swan. Quickly she clambered on to the swan's broad back and he swam strongly over the dark waters of the wide river. When they reached the opposite side the swan waddled up through the thick reeds and Gretel waved her magic wand again. The swan disappeared as quickly as it had come and there stood Hansel once again.

They were nearly home and just as the evening shadows lengthened and the sun began to sink, they arrived at their door. They rushed in and found their father sitting alone in his old chair. He was overjoyed at their return and the tears flowed down his kind old face as he wrapped his arms about them. Since he had left them in the forest he had not had a moment's peace. Such was the sorrow he felt at doing his wife's bidding that his heart had broken.

As for his wife? One day her stony heart had stopped beating and she had died. The woodsman had not shed a tear for her but since her death

had lived a solitary life, alone with his grief for his lost children.

Hansel then emptied out his pockets and Gretel did the same. The jewels and pearls tumbled on to the floor; the gold and silver coins chinked and clinked as they too fell all around, gleaming and glittering in the last glow of the evening sunset.

The woodsman's tired old eyes opened wide with amazement – they were rich at last! And from that day on their troubles were over and they lived happily ever after.

The Mule

THERE was once a mule who was as fat as a barrel; she ate too much and she ate too often. She jumped and clopped and kicked about, swishing her tail and exclaiming, 'My mother was a race-horse and I'm as fine as she.'

But, alas, all her weight and self-indulgence got the better of her and she collapsed, exhausted from her frisking. Only then did she remember that her father was an ass.

There are two sides to every coin.

The Peacock & the Crane

THE peacock preened and strutted, tossing his head this way and that and hardly acknowledging his fellows as he minced along. Suddenly, in the middle of his path, he happened to meet a crane. The crane paid no attention to the conceited bird but quietly continued with his business, dipping and pecking at the scattered seed on the ground.

Drawing himself up to his full height, the peacock looked at the crane with contempt. He displayed his beautiful tail feathers, hoping to shame the creature: 'Such a mean, ordinary bird!' he thought.

The crane, however, was not to be slighted quite so easily. He tilted his head to one side and said, 'You are indeed a very fine bird, at least your feathers paint you so, but surely it is better to fly high above the clouds on strong wings, than to strut about on the ground like a child's pretty plaything.'

Fine feathers do not make fine birds.

The Snow Queen

LONG AGO AT THE BEGINNING OF TIME the devil sat in his workshop and made an evil mirror. It reflected the beauty of the earth but when the devil looked into it all beauty vanished and turned into loathsome ugliness. The fresh-scented forests of pines became withered, slime-covered swamps; flowers turned black, crumpled up and died and butterflies lost their colour and became spiky, poisonous creatures. But worst of all was what the mirror did to a human face: no matter how beautiful, it was twisted and distorted into a hideous, misshapen mask.

The devil was pleased – the mirror would help his evil work. He took up the thigh-bone of a wolf and brought it down violently on to the mirror. It smashed into a million fragments and instantly a howl of wind screamed into the workshop. The wind whisked the splinters into the air and sent them spinning around the devil's head and he laughed out loud. The glass splinters tumbled and twisted and the devil laughed even louder. The louder he laughed the more the wind swirled the deadly slivers about his head. Soon he was laughing so loudly that the broken fragments were scattered like an evil whirlwind all round the world. Tiny pieces were blown into every nook and cranny, in all directions. They would do the devil's work – and he laughed even louder at the thought of the sorrow they would bring.

*   *   *

In the great city of Copenhagen lived a little girl called Gerda. She was very poor, and apart from the love of her parents, had nothing to brighten her life except the friendship of her neighbour, Kai. His house was right next door to hers and they loved each other like brother and sister. They were never happier than when they were together.

The two families lived high up in the attics right under the roofs of the houses. These were so close that apart from a thin strip of sky, they

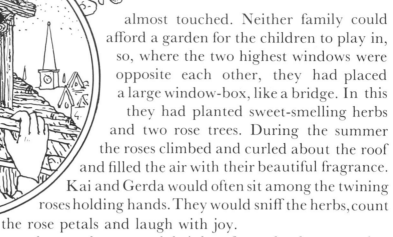

almost touched. Neither family could
afford a garden for the children to play in,
so, where the two highest windows were
opposite each other, they had placed
a large window-box, like a bridge. In this
they had planted sweet-smelling herbs
and two rose trees. During the summer
the roses climbed and curled about the roof
and filled the air with their beautiful fragrance.
Kai and Gerda would often sit among the twining
roses holding hands. They would sniff the herbs, count
the rose petals and laugh with joy.

The days were long and warm and their love for each other grew, day
by day, just like the climbing roses.

When Winter came and set his hand over the city, the children could
no longer play in their garden; all the windows were bolted tight against
the chill winds that beat upon them. The children would then take a
coin, warmed by the fire, and hold it against the window-pane. The
frost would melt in a tiny circle and each would peer through at the
other, laughing all the while. The snow fell and piled high in the streets
below and they longed to be together again but, until the snow melted,
they could only peep through the tiny holes in the frosty glass. At last,
the long spiky icicles would start to drip and the snows melt. Spring was
coming and soon they would be together again in their garden.

Once again the warmth of the sun fell on them, and once again their
love grew sweet as the roses twining above them. One sunny day a
butterfly settled on Kai's finger. As the children wondered at its beauty,
Kai gave a start: 'Ouch,' he said, pulling a face and clutching at his
breast. The butterfly fluttered into the branches above them. 'That
hurt, whatever . . . Ouch!' A second time Kai cried out and this time he
rubbed at his eye. 'Something's hurt my eye, now!' he said.

'Let me look,' said Gerda and her eyes were wide with care as she
reached towards him.

'No, leave me be,' snapped Kai and he pushed her away. It was the
devil's splinters and they had entered his heart and his eye. Kai had
never treated Gerda so roughly before and she started to cry.

'Oh, don't start blubbering,' said Kai. 'You look so ugly when you
cry.' He stood up and trampled on the new green herbs under his feet.
'I'm fed up with this place,' he scoffed. 'Look at that worm-eaten rose,

. . . and there's another. I'm going!'
He kicked at the window-box and
stamped away leaving Gerda alone to
her quiet tears in their broken garden.

Winter came again and the city was
covered once more in a white blanket of
snow. Each night Gerda made a peephole in
her window, but whenever she saw Kai, he
would turn away. She knew he still looked from
his window, but now, it was never for her. It was as
if she had become a stranger . . .

One night the snow was falling heavily, swirling and tumbling in the
gusty wind. Kai watched the snowflakes pile up on his window-sill, one
on top of the other and as he watched them settle, they formed
themselves into strange shapes. He looked more closely and before his
eyes the outline of a face began to form. He could just make out a pair of
deepset eyes beneath a high brow, a finely-chiselled nose and the thin
line of beautiful lips. The face seemed to be looking straight at him and
suddenly it came to life. Although a little afraid, Kai thought the face
very beautiful. The finely-drawn lips smiled at him but the smile had no
warmth in it – it was as cold as the frost of the darkest night.

The next day Kai felt bored. He didn't know what to do and was tired
of staying indoors. Finally, he asked his grandmother if he might take
his sled to the square to play with the other town boys. His tone was cross
and his face sullen.

'And Gerda,' she asked. 'Is she going too?'

Kai gave a sneer and walked over to the door and began to put on his
coat and gloves. 'I won't be playing with her,' he said. 'She is just a silly
child. She spends her time moaning and crying.' The door slammed and
he was gone. From her window Gerda watched him trudge through the
snow, dragging his little sled behind him. She felt a deep sorrow pierce
her heart – it seemed he no longer loved her.

In the square the tall buildings echoed as the town boys called to each
other, sliding back and forth on their sleds. Many of them held on to
passing carts to hitch a free ride, letting go just as the cart was about to
leave the square. Kai ran to join them and almost immediately a long
white sled pulled by two grey horses glided past him. The driver sat high
up in the front and was dressed from top to toe in the palest blue coat,
trimmed with the whitest fur Kai had ever seen. He watched as it

silently swished around the square and then, as it passed again, he leapt forward and tied his sled behind it.

Away they went at a fine speed. Kai hung on and laughed with delight as his little sled bumped and hissed through the thick snow. But then the big white sled began to move faster and turned to leave the square: it was heading straight for the city gates. Kai tried to untie the knot that bound the two sleds together but his fingers were numb and slow and he was forced to hold on even tighter lest he be thrown off and injured. He cried out but no-one seemed to hear.

Faster and faster went the great sled and it seemed to Kai that they were flying through the snowdrifts. His teeth began to chatter and just when he thought he was about to fall, the great sled glided softly to a stop. Kai slumped down on his sled, exhausted.

The driver turned and for the first time Kai saw the face of a beautiful woman. Her skin was smooth and white and her eyes were an icy blue. She was looking down at him and Kai thought she reminded him of someone else. Was it the way she smiled? Where had he seen her before? he thought. Then he remembered the face in the snow. The face that he had seen outside his window. It was the Snow Queen!

She stepped down from her high seat and placed a hand on his shoulder. A chill ran through his body and he shivered.

'Are you cold, Kai?' she asked and she leant to kiss him. Her lips were as cold as ice and Kai felt a pain as sharp as a frozen needle stab through to his heart. When the chill of her kiss seeped through to the devil's splinter he felt the cold no longer. He was as ice himself.

'Come,' said the Snow Queen. 'Climb up beside me.'

Kai could not believe how beautiful she was and wondered why he had thought her so cold and aloof; he had no doubts or fears now. He no longer cared where they were going and gave no thought to his home or his grandmother. He did not remember the roses or the love of his dear friend Gerda – all were now forgotten.

Swish went the sled across the icy wastes and then, rising into the air, it flew high above the ground. Kai looked down through the crisp, dark night and the dancing snowflakes: oceans and plains, snow-covered forests and jagged, white-topped mountains passed beneath him. Far below he heard the howling of wolves like the screech of the wind in his ears. They flew across a land of tumbling glaciers and black, cold waters until, at last, wrapped in the pure white fur of the Snow Queen's cloak, he fell into an icy sleep.

Meanwhile, in her tiny room, Gerda watched and waited for Kai's return. She had climbed up on her window seat and had sat there for hours peering through the frosty glass. At last, when he did not return, her tears began to fall. Oh, how she cried for her dear lost friend. Where had he gone?

The townsfolk said that by now he must have perished in the cold. Some of them had seen him leave the city behind the great white sled. Perhaps it had crashed through the ice while crossing the nearby river. Gerda's heart was full of sadness and each day, until the Spring returned once more, she watched from her window.

Then, as the first weak threads of early sunshine brushed her face she felt warm again. 'My poor Kai must surely be dead,' she murmured. But the sunbeams heard her soft voice and answered: 'It is not so. It is not so.'

The swallows swept and dived about her head and again Gerda said sadly: 'Do you not know, my poor Kai is dead.'

'It is not so. It is not so,' they answered.

'Perhaps,' said Gerda, taking heart 'my love is still alive. I will ask the river what it knows. I will wear my new red shoes for Kai has never seen them. I'm sure he'll think them pretty.'

So Gerda put on the red shoes. They were simple and plain, but because she was so poor, she thought them beautiful and treasured them greatly. She crept downstairs and out of the house, crossed the great square and walked through the city gates. After a while she reached the wide river. It gurgled and swirled at her feet and she stood for a while watching the curling reeds waving under the clear water.

Gerda knelt down on the bank and looking deep into the water she asked: 'Do you know if my Kai is alive? Please, if you can bring him back to me, I will give you my new red shoes.'

The river sighed and Gerda thought she saw the reeds and the waters nod to her question. She unbuckled her shoes and threw them into the river. She was not very strong and her throw had cast them only a short way from the bank. The tiny waves lapped at the reeds and the shoes floated back as if the river was returning them to her.

'I have not thrown them far enough,' she said and looking round she saw a boat nestling among the rushes. She climbed in and raising her arm high, she threw the shoes into the river again. This time they did not float back to her but her movement rocked the little boat and it began to move. Slowly, but surely, it drifted out from the bank. Gerda ran to the

back of the boat but it was too late: it was already too far for
her to jump to safety. There was nothing she could do.

Gerda huddled fearfully in the spinning boat as it moved faster and
faster. She drew up her knees and hugged herself but then the swallows
came again. 'Do not cry,' they said. 'We are with you, don't be
frightened.'

Their voices made her feel better and she sat up and looked around.
She was drifting through a land of green willow trees and tall rushes,
dipping and swaying in the warm summer breeze. Wild flowers,
sparkling like coloured jewels, speckled the gently waving grasses of the
meadow.

'Perhaps I am being taken to Kai,' she thought and she smiled quietly
to herself.

For many hours the boat drifted along on the rippling water. Gerda
sat and watched the scenery glide past but suddenly she saw a tiny
cottage. It had a pointed roof and two small windows made from
coloured glass. Strangest of all, however, were two wooden soldiers
standing on either side of the doorway. Gerda called out to them and
they saluted but they did not answer. Fearful that she would be carried
right past the cottage she called out again. This time her cry brought an

old lady to the cottage doorway. She came over to the bank, took hold of the boat with her long crooked stick and drew it safely into the reeds.

'Why my poor little love,' she said. 'What are you doing so far from home?' The old lady was tall and thin, and on her head she wore a huge straw hat completely covered with flowers. They danced and played around its brim as she bobbed her head up and down. Gerda took her hand and jumped out of the boat. She felt a little uneasy as the old lady led her up to the cottage.

'Do you have a story to tell, my dear?' she asked, and Gerda told her of her search for Kai and of her long journey down the river. She then asked the old lady if she had seen Kai.

'Not yet, my pet,' replied the old lady. 'But he may pass my door some day and pay me a visit.' The lady clapped her hands together: 'Now,' she said 'would you like something to eat? I have some cherries that are ripe and fresh and, afterwards you can see my garden. I have such lovely flowers planted there and should you ask them, each will tell you a different story.'

Gerda entered the cottage and found a large bowl of cherries. She began to eat them. The sunshine darted through the coloured glass of the window-panes and made pretty patterns of red, blue and yellow all over the walls.

The old lady went to a drawer and took out a comb, then she began to comb Gerda's hair. 'You are a pretty child,' she cooed. 'Such fine hair is rightly fit for my golden comb. A child like you has been my heart's desire. We shall surely come to love each other.'

Gerda felt soothed by the old lady's soft voice and gentle stroking. She had eaten her fill and now her thoughts drifted away from her beloved Kai. She closed her eyes and listened to the soft buzz of the afternoon. She felt warm and drowsy and slipped into a light sleep.

The old woman was, indeed, a witch. But her magic was only used for good and not for evil; it had worked very well. She thought it very fortunate that Gerda had been brought to her door, now all she needed was to make sure that Gerda stayed with her. 'I must make the child forget about her young friend, Kai,' she murmured. And while Gerda slept the old lady went into her garden. She went straight to the rosebush and sweeping her stick over it, she whispered a magic charm. Instantly, the roses disappeared: the other plants closed up, leaving no trace of where the rose-bush had been. 'Now there is no flower in the garden to remind her of Kai,' she said.

When Gerda awoke the old lady led her out of the house into the garden. The sun was shining and Gerda was astonished at how beautiful it was. She had never seen so many flowers and she knelt and played among them. Her heart was filled with delight at the sight of so much colour and the scent of so many sweet perfumes.

One day followed another and Gerda spent all of her time in the enchanted garden among the flowers. But a tiny doubt had entered her mind. 'They are not all here,' she said. 'But which flower is missing? I wish I could remember.'

That evening, as the old lady sat in her large wicker chair, dozing contentedly, Gerda suddenly looked up and gasped. 'The rose!' she cried, pointing at the old lady's hat. 'That's the one that's missing!'

'Oh my, Oh my . . .' began the old lady, but it was too late: Gerda had seen the one single rose that had escaped the old lady's spell. Gerda realised at once that she had been deceived. She ran from the cottage and sank to her knees in the garden. She was so upset that she began to cry. Her tears fell to the ground and touched the spot where the rose bush had once bloomed, instantly they sprang back to life. Gerda was overcome with joy. Taking a rose in her hand she wept bitterly: 'Oh Kai, I so nearly forgot you. I have wasted my time with flowers when I should have been searching for you.' She looked closely into the warm heart of the rose and asked: 'Is my dear Kai alive? Have you seen him?'

The rose in her hand seemed to shiver: 'No, I have not seen him and I know only too well of death, but nothing of Kai. He is surely alive.' Gerda ran from flower to flower and asked them all the same question. 'Is Kai alive? Is Kai alive? Have you seen him?' She heard many stories and strange tales but all of them turned away at her question and said they knew nothing of him.

'I cannot stop and listen to your tales,' cried Gerda. 'I must find Kai.' And she ran from the garden and out through the gate. Finally, exhausted, she sank down to the ground and fell into a deep sleep.

When she awoke she shivered and hugged herself, it had grown quite chilly. Then she heard a strange sound.

'Coo-roo, . . . roo, roo! Coo-roo, . . . roo, roo!' There it was again. Just then a leaf fluttered down and landed in her lap; she looked up and there, perched in the branches of a tree, was a fat wood-pigeon.

'Hello,' she said. 'Is it Autumn already?'

'Why, yes,' said the pigeon. Then Gerda remembered the garden; it was enchanted. No seasons affected the flowers there, no frosts drove the

plants underground for the winter, it had always been summer. 'Please, have you seen Kai?' she asked and her voice was urgent. The pigeon paused and looked thoughtful, then he said sadly: 'Yes, I have seen him . . .' His voice trailed off in a murmur. Gerda thought he was about to cry and fearing the worst she blurted out: 'Is Kai dead?'

'No, he's alive. I was here by my nest a winter ago and I saw him pass overhead. He was with the Snow Queen in her sled.' Once again the pigeon paused. 'As she flew by,' he went on, 'she breathed an icy kiss on my young ones and they perished . . . every one.'

The pigeon gulped and looked away. Gerda waited for a moment and then she asked in a softer voice: 'Where were they going? I must find Kai.' The pigeon shuffled his feet before answering.

'To Lappland. It's a long way from here, to the North . . . and very cold. I'm afraid I don't know the way, but if you ask the reindeer they'll be sure to tell you. Go north from here, only a short distance, and you'll come to the land where they live.' Gerda thanked him and set off. She left the pigeon sadly staring off into the distance.

The further North she went the colder it got. Patches of snow dotted the ground and Gerda's feet became frosty blue. At last she saw a reindeer scratching his back against a fallen tree-trunk.

The reindeer, who had a kind face, listened patiently while Gerda told him her story. When she had finished he said that he would take her on his back to the land of the Snow Queen.

'Does she live in Lappland?' asked Gerda.

'Only in the summer,' answered the reindeer. 'Her winter palace lies far away to the north in a land of darkness and lights. Where the ice never melts and the wind cuts through you like a knife.'

Gerda climbed on to his broad back. 'It's getting cold,' he said. 'You'd better snuggle as deep as you can into my thick fur.'

Off they went across the wide plain. The land grew white with frost and cold as ice. The reindeer galloped on and on and did not seem to notice the icy winds and tumbling snowstorms. All the while Gerda hugged herself closer and closer into his broad shoulders.

At last he came to a stop beside a ragged hut, its roof piled high with snow. The reindeer snorted two great puffs of steam and Gerda looked up. She could see the warm glow of a lamp shining from a tiny window. The door opened and an old Lapp woman peeped out. 'Come inside, it's cold,' she said, and the reindeer trotted into the hut.

He told the old Lapp woman Gerda's story. When he had finished she got up and fetched a bowl of steaming soup for Gerda and some fresh straw for the reindeer. After they had eaten she pulled a thick fur about her knees and began to talk. 'Kai is living with the Snow Queen. He is deep inside her palace and he is content. To him it is the most beautiful place on earth. He does not feel the chill in his bones or the frost on his face. His heart is filled with ice and he is happy there. Unless the magic that has entered his eye and his heart is destroyed, he will never know what it is to be human again.'

Gerda was near to tears when she heard the old woman's words. It seemed she had lost Kai's love forever.

'But what magic can bring him back, old woman?' asked the kindly reindeer, cocking his great antlers to one side. 'What can Gerda do?'

'There is no magic,' said the Lapp woman. 'It is the warmth of Gerda's love that will bring Kai back from his frozen life. Has she not

travelled far in the hope of finding him? Has she not trusted the birds of
the air and the flowers of the field to guide her way? Such a faithful love
is all that can release him from his icy tomb.'

'It is still far away,' said the reindeer, 'but I will take you to the gates
of the palace. I can go no further, or I too, will perish.'

The next morning at dawn, the old Lapp woman dressed Gerda in a
warm fur suit. Then she kissed her goodbye and they set off once more
across the frozen ice.

Gerda had never seen so much ice. It twisted and tilted in crackling
mountains of blue and white. The snow danced in a frenzy and the wind
screamed about their ears. The closer they got to the Snow Queen's
palace, the colder it became, until, finally, when it seemed the very air
itself was frozen, the reindeer stopped.

'We are here at last,' he said and his voice was tired and weary.

'Thank you dear friend,' said Gerda, and leaning forward, she kissed
him on top of his nose. The reindeer looked sad. 'Good luck, Gerda,' he
whispered.

Gerda left him at the palace gates. As she turned to wave two tears fell
from his large brown eyes and rolled down his shaggy cheeks.

Inside the palace the corridors and caverns glistened and sparkled. Icy creakings echoed through the bone-chilled chambers. Deep in its cold heart was the Snow Queen's throne room. There, seated on a throne of ice, encrusted with the frozen tears of a million sadnesses, sat the Snow Queen. Her gown was the colour of the bluest iceberg, trimmed with frozen jewels as black as the polar sea; on her head she wore a crown of splintered ice needles.

On the floor at her feet sat Kai. He was playing with a pile of ice fragments, making up words: ICE, CHILL, DARKNESS, COLD . . . over and over again he spelt out the words. His hair was frosty white and his face and hands were an icy black. He was as cold as the Snow Queen's smile but he felt nothing. His brittle fingers toyed with the splinters, one word eluded him but his memory for it was lost.

The Snow Queen had once told him of the word, it was ETERNITY: she had promised him his freedom if he found it among the fragments. But now, his fingers were so numb and his mind so frozen, that he could not remember a single letter.

Suddenly, the Snow Queen stood up and clapped her hands. Instantly her glistening sled appeared before her. She smiled at Kai as she stepped into her high seat. 'I am going away for a while,' she said. 'I must tend to the snows on the tops of the volcanos. Their warmth is sometimes strong enough to melt the thickest ice and I must breathe on them again and cap them in white.'

The sled hissed from the chamber and the crack of her whip echoed through the palace like a thousand snapping icicles. Kai was left alone, all was silent except for the tiny clinking of the ice splinters falling between his frozen fingers.

*　　　*　　　*

Gerda entered the chamber and the chill air cut through her cloak and gnawed at her bones. Then she saw the tiny figure by the throne. 'Kai,' she called. 'At last I've found you. It's me, dearest friend, Gerda.'

Kai turned but his face gave no sign of warmth. His cold blue eyes seemed not to know her. He did not move and his hands remained frozen at his side.

Gerda flung her arms around him and wept. 'It's me, It's me, Kai,' and the tears fell from her eyes. She felt the icy chill of his shoulders against her and the frozen stiffness of his body seeped through her thick fur suit. There was no response; it was as if he had no love for her at all. In despair, Gerda lowered her head to his breast and sobbed bitterly.

Her tears were warm and full of love and, falling on his breast, they
entered his heart. The evil splinters melted in the flood of her love. She
felt Kai stir; he stood back, holding her away from him as if to see her
more clearly.

Gerda would have collapsed had he not held her shoulders. She
looked sadly at him with eyes full of love and warmth. She had longed
for him so much all through her long journey and now her tears ran
freely down her cheeks. 'It's Gerda. Don't you remember the roses?' and
her sad voice was like a tiny sunbeam.

At that moment the warmth in Kai's heart flowed into his memory.
Thoughts of their childhood came flooding back to him: it was Gerda!
Seeing her dear face in front of him as if for the first time, his eyes filled
with tears. He clasped her to him and cried so freely that his eye was
washed clean of the devil's second splinter. He could see now the beauty
of her smile and the dark ugliness all around him; he felt alive and he
shivered as he became aware of the cold.

Gerda kissed him and kissed him and with every kiss more warmth flowed into his cold body. Their tears mingled and fell to the floor on to the ice splinters that lay there. Some of them were melted and some of them were frozen into new letters. Kai glanced down and saw the word ETERNITY. 'We are free, my love,' he said.

*   *   *

Full of joy they ran from the palace, out through the frozen gates and on to the snow-covered wasteland outside. The terrible wind now seemed to be quieter and as they walked along a faint gleam of sunshine broke through the clouds and warmed their faces. They reached the top of a tumbling snowdrift and Gerda smiled: 'Hello, old friend,' she said. It was the reindeer.

'I, . . . I thought I'd wait around for a while,' he muttered. 'Just in case I was needed.'

Together they climbed on to his broad back and set off for their home. It was a long way, but strangely the cold did not now chill them. The sun came out and in no time at all the snows had disappeared and they were riding into a green meadow. Here, the reindeer set them down and bade farewell. This time he smiled as he watched them go on their way.

Soon Kai and Gerda discarded their warm fur coats. The sun was shining and the sky seemed full of swallows. They darted and played, swooping down around the heads of the young couple.

'Did we not say. It was true. It was true,' they whispered.

At last they saw in the distance the tall towers and steeples of Copenhagen. With their hands locked together they turned and looked into each other's eyes. No warmth could match the love they felt for each other. 'Remember our roses?' said Kai gently, and he kissed her tenderly on the lips.

They were no longer children, but had grown, as had their love.

The Lark
& the Farmer

A BLUE sky covered the countryside and the warm sun was slowly turning the cornfields to gold. In one such field there lived a lark and her family of young chicks. Their nest was hidden beneath the tall shoots and the birds lived there happily.

Above their heads the ripe grain weighed heavily on the bending stalks which swayed in the warm summer breeze. The mother lark, at this time of year, was especially attentive: each day she listened for the sound of the reapers and warned her young family to mind each sight and sound. They should tell her straightaway if they heard or saw anything strange, for when the reaping was about to start they would have to find a new home.

As the days passed the young larks skittered and dived among the tall grasses surrounding the field, hiding and swooping, one moment in sunshine, the next in shadow. One morning a man's voice interrupted their play and they came close together in a silently listening group.

'It is full time,' said the man. It was the farmer and he stood only a pace away from them, feeling the ears of corn between his hard brown fingers. 'I must call in the neighbours to help reap my corn,' he added.

The youngsters waited until the man had turned away, then they fled to their mother with the news and begged her to take them safely away.

'Time enough, my featherlings,' she comforted. 'If the farmer trusts to the help of his neighbours he will wait a long time for his harvest.' And so saying she settled her chicks under her wing for the night.

A few more days of sunshine passed and the farmer came again, this time standing very close to their nest. Now he was accompanied by his tall and eager son.

'Still nothing done and this corn's ripe and ready,' he said. 'We cannot depend on our neighbours, we'll call up our uncles and cousins to help.'

The young larks trembled once more because he had been so close, but their mother reassured them: 'Don't be frightened, the uncles and

200

cousins have fields of their own, so they'll not come, you mark my words.' She paused and straightened a feather, then drawing her babes about her she added quietly, 'But listen carefully, my chicks, to the next words he says.'

The farmer and his son stood in the field again two days later. ''Tis falling, and no-one at work,' said the farmer, his face dark with concern. 'We must wait for our friends and relations no longer, my lad. We'll sharpen our sickles and reap it ourselves – tomorrow; there's no time to lose!'

The chicks had been listening with bated breath and now they flew to their mother as fast as they could; they cheeped and hopped about excitedly as they waited for her to speak.

'Indeed,' she said, 'it's time to be off. If the farmer now means to do it himself instead of waiting for others, you may be sure that he will work at it hard until it's done.' And without more ado she urged them aloft to seek a new home.

If you want something done then do it yourself.

Rumpelstiltskin

ONCE THERE LIVED A MILLER: he was not too bright and not too rich, but he did so want to get on in the world. He would tell his friends the tallest tales of how clever he was; how much gold he had, and how many fine clothes he possessed. Unfortunately no one ever saw his oft-proclaimed wealth for no one was ever invited into his house. What little money he had was spent on clothes, to impress his neighbours, but they never quite looked right; his legs were too short and his belly was too fat, so nothing ever fitted. Try as he might he never managed to look like a proper gentleman. He did, however, have one very important asset – he had a very beautiful daughter!

Now it happened that one day the king was passing by close to the millhouse. The miller rushed out, bowing and scraping, with his shirt bursting out behind him from underneath his bulging waistcoat. The king paused, but his eyes were not on the miller but on the miller's daughter who was standing by the door.

When he perceived the king's attention, however, the red-faced miller smiled the more. As usual, he said too much, and before he could stop himself he blurted out: "Yes, my lord, a fine girl indeed . . . and so clever! Why, she can even spin straw into the finest gold."

The king was not impressed with the bragging miller's tale and looked disdainfully down from his horse. "My good fellow, that is surely a rare talent! Tomorrow you must bring her to the palace that I may witness your amazing claim."

The miller gulped – what had he said now! But just as he was bade he took his daughter the very next day to the king's palace. The girl stood patiently before the king while her father fawned and feinted, doffing his cap so often that his wig became lopsided on his shiny bald head.

Ignoring the miller's constant chatter the king stepped down from his throne and led the girl to a chamber filled with straw in which stood a

spinning wheel and a pile of bobbins.

"Now spin this straw to gold," he commanded. "If, from now till dawn, you cannot use all the straw and turn it into gold, then you will die." He closed the door and locked her in.

The miller's daughter was beside herself with anguish. She had not the slightest idea how to spin straw into gold and in despair she burst into tears. How could she justify her father's stupid claim!

As darkness came, her sobbing continued unabated. Then, quite suddenly, the door sprang open and in scampered a strange little man. "How now, my pretty miller's maid, why do you weep so woefully?"

The miller's daughter dried her eyes. "I've to spin this straw into gold by dawn or I must surely die, and truly sir, I have no way to do it."

The little man busily hopped from one foot to the other.

"We'll see, we'll see . . . what can be done. What gift will you give if I spin the straw to glittering gold?"

"You may have my necklace," said the girl raising her delicate hand to her throat. Without more ado the little man leaped to the spinning wheel and sat himself down. Round it flew and round again, and then once more a third time. There – in front of him was a bobbin of gold! All through the night the wheel whirled round and round and didn't stop till dawn when all the straw was gone and in its place was shining gold.

When shortly after, the king unlocked the door, his mouth fell open in surprise. So much gold, he thought, what a treasure have I found in this fair maid. Such wealth was easy to come by, and more was for the taking. That evening he took the miller's daughter to a much larger chamber, again it was full of straw and there sat the spinning wheel and bobbins. He repeated his command of the previous day and once more locked her

in. Again she wept but this time not for long, for no sooner had dusk descended than the little man appeared. "How now, what pleasing present will you give if I spin the straw to strands of shining gold?"

The maiden raised her milk-white hand. "This gold ring upon my finger," she answered. At once the little man set to work, the wheel whirling round and round through the night until the very last strip of straw had been spun into gold.

The king was delighted with the night's work. He clapped his hands and had all the gold bobbins carried to his coffers. But his greed for more had grown even stronger: if the maid continued with her work forever more, he'd surely be the richest king in all the land. He straightaway ordered that the great hall be cleared and filled instead with as much straw as it would hold. It was the largest room within the palace and it took nearly all day to fill it up with straw. The wheel was placed inside the door and the miller's daughter again locked in for the night. She sat within the great hall, pensively thinking on the king's last words. "Tomorrow," he had said. "If all the straw is spun into gold by dawn, then I will make you my wife . . . you will be my queen."

"Fancy?" she murmured. "A humble miller's daughter – a queen!" But then, for the third time the little man appeared before her and asked, as usual, what she would give him for his work. The miller's daughter was forlorn and when she spoke her voice was merely a whisper. "Alas sir, I am sorry, but I have nothing left to reward you for your labour."

The little man scratched his head and raised his bushy eyebrows. "Well now, my miller's maid, this is a puzzling problem. But you'll be quickly queen and then, perchance, a child you'll cherish. Your promise I will take – the baby born will be mine!"

"I cannot say that it surely will be," she answered softly, "but if it happens to be so, then you have my promise."

Once more the spinning wheel whirled and the straw flew through the little man's nimble fingers. Soon the entire hall was shining with piles of gleaming golden bobbins.

In the morning the king was as good as his word: finding all the straw gone and the great hall full of gold, he gave orders for a wedding feast to be prepared. He would marry the miller's daughter.

They lived happily in the palace and the king had so much gold that he no longer asked his wife to sit and spin – besides, he had run out of places to store it all.

A year passed by, and then another, and the queen gave birth to a child – a baby daughter. The child was so delightful that she instantly became the apple of the king's eye and the queen's heart was full of joy. But just three days after the child's birth, she remembered her promise to the strange little man. Hardly had the thought entered her head when he appeared in the room beside her.

"A promise promised is a promise kept," he said. "You must now give me the child. The queen began to weep and begged him not to take the baby girl, offering instead to give him all the riches she possessed. The tiny figure just repeated his request, but her pathetic tears softened his heart and he relented.

"Three days have I waited, so three more shall you have. Within that length of time – today, tomorrow and the third – you must find my name. Should you guess right the pretty princess will be yours."

The queen was greatly comforted by this reprieve but her heart beat wildly as she wracked her brain to remember all the names she'd ever heard. The little man returned that very same evening and asked her for her thoughts.

"Is your name John, or Jack, or is it Lancelot?" she asked, but to each and every name she mentioned the little man solemnly shook his head.

The next day the queen asked her servants what names they knew and sent guards to scour the countryside; they were ordered to seek out every name that ever was. Again the little man appeared at dusk and bade her speak his name.

"Is it Aaron, Arnold, Arthur, Axel . . .?" Again he shook his head.

The third day dawned, it was the last, and the queen felt in her heart that all was lost. However, one of her guards had travelled far away to the mountains. He went straight to the queen to tell her of a strange occurrence he had witnessed close by a lonely cottage.

Outside the house a fire blazed and dancing around it was a strange little man, hopping from one foot to the other. The guard had concealed himself behind a thicket to watch yet not be seen and the little man had started to sing. He sang the same song over and over again, and his words had made the guard prick up his ears.

> "I'll bake and brew, tomorrow too,
> But then, princess, I'll come for you.
> It's such a shame the queen can't claim
> That Rumpelstiltskin is my name!"

It must surely be him thought the queen when she heard the guard's news and she thanked him warmly for his help. That evening the little man appeared for the last time.

"How now, good queen, what is my name?"

The queen pretended to be puzzled and pulled thoughtfully at her lip. "Be it James? Or is it Robert? Be it Gabriel or Ben?" She spoke lightly and waited for the little man to shake his head. He did so and she smiled.

"Then it must be Rumpelstiltskin!"

The little man's face grew purple with anger and he clenched his little fists together and jumped up and down in a fearful rage. "Who told you? Who told you? It surely was the devil!" His temper boiled and boiled and he hopped up and down so wildly that he began to fall to pieces. Each piece in turn hopped about and flew in all directions – through the door and out of the windows: and, from that day to this he's never been seen again – nor, for that matter, have any of the pieces.

The Dog & the Bone

A WIRY dog, of doubtful reputation, was swaggering home one day when he happened to pass a butcher's shop. Seeing a pile of tasty bones on the counter he greedily snatched one and ran off.

Later, as he went on his way, he crossed a river. Half-way over the bridge he chanced to see his reflection in the water below him. Thinking that it was another dog, and one with an equally tasty meal in its mouth, he resolved to make himself master of the situation.

He growled and snapped at the dog in the water, opening his jaws wide to show off his sharp fangs and so frighten his enemy. Immediately the bone fell from his mouth and plopped into the stream where it sank to the bottom – out of his reach and lost forever.

Be content with what you have.

The Boy Who Cried Wolf

O N a hill above a village stood a young shepherd boy. He was bored and so, to amuse himself, he cried out to the village below: 'The wolf! The wolf! The wolf is coming!'

His trick succeeded. Three times the villagers came panting up the steep hillside to help him save his sheep. Each time, when they reached him, the boy just laughed and they felt cheated and angry.

Alas, for the boy, one grey misty day the wolf really did come, and straightaway the beast set about the sheep. The boy cried out in earnest: 'The wolf is here! Help me! The wolf is here!'

No-one answered his call for the villagers thought it just another of his tricks – and the wolf devoured all his sheep.

The boy had learned his lesson too late, that liars are not often believed even when they do tell the truth.

The Butterfly
that Stamped

THIS, O my Best Beloved, is a story – a new and a wonderful story– a story quite different from the other stories – a story about The Most Wise Sovereign-Suleiman-bin-Daoud – Solomon the Son of David.

There are three hundred and fifty-five stories about Suleiman-bin-Daoud; but this is not one of them. It is not the story of the Lapwing who found the Water; or the Hoopoe who shaded Suleiman-bin-Daoud from the heat. It is not the story of the Glass Pavement, or the Ruby with the Crooked Hole, or the Gold Bars of Balkis. It is the story of the Butterfly that Stamped.

Now attend all over again and listen!

Suleiman-bin-Daoud was wise. He understood what the beasts said, what the birds said, what the fishes said, and what the insects said. He understood what the rocks said deep under the earth when they bowed in towards each other and groaned: and he understood what the trees said when they rustled in the middle of the morning. He understood everything, from the bishop on the bench to the hyssop on the wall; and Balkis, his Head Queen, the Most Beautiful Queen Balkis, was nearly as wise as he was.

Suleiman-bin-Daoud was strong. Upon the third finger of his right hand he wore a ring. When he turned it once, Afrits and Djinns came out of the earth to do whatever he told them. When he turned it twice, Fairies came down from the sky to do whatever he told them; and when he turned it three times, the very great angel Azrael of the Sword came dressed as a water-carrier, and told him the news of the three worlds, – Above – Below – and Here.

And yet Suleiman-bin-Daoud was not proud. He very seldom showed off, and when he did he was sorry for it. Once he tried to feed all the animals in all the world in one day, but when the food was ready an Animal came out of the deep sea and ate it up in three mouthfuls. Suleiman-bin-Daoud was very surprised and said 'O Animal, who are you?' And the Animal said, 'O King, live for ever! I am the smallest of

An Animal came out of the deep deep sea and ate it all up

thirty thousand brothers, and our home is at the bottom of the sea. We heard that you were going to feed all the animals in all the world, and my brothers sent me to ask when dinner would be ready.' Suleiman-bin-Daoud was more surprised then ever and said, 'O Animal, you have eaten all the dinner that I made ready for all the animals in the world.' And the Animal said, 'O King, live for ever, but do you really call *that* a dinner? Where I come from we each eat twice as much as that between meals.' Then Suleiman-bin-Daoud fell flat on his face and said, 'O Animal! I gave that dinner to show what a great and rich king I was, and not because I really wanted to be kind to the animals. Now I am ashamed, and it serves me right.' Suleiman-bin-Daoud was a really truly wise man, Best Beloved. After that he never forgot that it was silly to show off; and now the real story part of my story begins.

He married ever so many wives. He married nine hundred and ninety-nine wives, besides the Most Beautiful Balkis; and they all lived in a great golden palace in the middle of a lovely garden with fountains. He didn't really want nine hundred and ninety-nine wives, but in those days everybody married ever so many wives, and of course the King had to marry ever so many more just to show that he was the King.

Some of the wives were nice, but some were simply horrid, and the horrid ones quarrelled with the nice ones and made them horrid too, and then they would all quarrel with Suleiman-bin-Daoud, and that was horrid for him. But Balkis the Most Beautiful never quarrelled with Suleiman-bin-Daoud. She loved him too much. She sat in her rooms in the Golden Palace, or walked in the Palace garden, and was truly sorry for him.

Of course if he had chosen to turn his ring on his finger and call up the Djinns and the Afrits they would have magicked all those nine hundred and ninety-nine quarrelsome wives into white mules of the desert or greyhounds or pomegranate seeds; but Suleiman-bin-Daoud thought that that would be showing off. So, when they quarrelled too much, he only walked by himself in one part of the beautiful Palace gardens and wished he had never been born.

One day, when they had quarrelled for three weeks – all nine hundred and ninety-nine wives together – Suleiman-bin-Daoud went out for peace and quiet as usual; and among the orange-trees he met Balkis the Most Beautiful, very sorrowful because Suleiman-bin-Daoud was so worried. And she said to him, 'O my Lord and Light of my Eyes, turn the ring upon your finger and show these Queens of Egypt and Mesopotamia and Persia and China that you are the great and terrible King.' But Suleiman-bin-Daoud shook his head and said, 'O my Lady and Delight of my Life, remember the Animal that came out of the sea and made me ashamed before all the animals in all the world because I showed off. Now, if I showed off before these Queens of Persia and Egypt and Abyssinia and China, merely because they worry me, I might be made even more ashamed than I have been.'

And Balkis the Most Beautiful said, 'O my Lord and Treasure of my soul, what will you do?'

And Suleiman-bin-Daoud said, 'O my Lady and Content of my Heart, I shall continue to endure my fate at the hands of these nine hundred and ninety-nine Queens who vex me with their continual quarrelling.'

So he went on between the lilies and the loquats and the roses and the cannas and the heavy-scented ginger-plants that grew in the garden, till

he came to the great camphor-tree that was called the Camphor-Tree of Suleiman-bin-Daoud. But Balkis hid among the tall irises and the spotted bamboos and the red lilies behind the camphor-tree, so as to be near her own true love, Suleiman-bin-Daoud.

Presently two Butterflies flew under the tree, quarrelling.

Suleiman-bin-Daoud heard one say to the other, 'I wonder at your presumption in talking like this to me. Don't you know that if I stamped with my foot all Suleiman-bin-Daoud's Palace and this garden here would immediately vanish in a clap of thunder?'

Then Suleiman-bin-Daoud forgot his nine hundred and ninety-nine bothersome wives, and laughed, till the camphor-tree shook, at the Butterfly's boast. And he held out his finger and said, 'Little man, come here.'

The Butterfly was dreadfully frightened, but he managed to fly up to the hand of Suleiman-bin-Daoud, and clung there, fanning himself. Suleiman-bin-Daoud bent his head and whispered very softly, 'Little man, you know that all your stamping wouldn't bend one blade of grass. What made you tell that awful fib to your wife? – for doubtless she is your wife.'

The Butterfly looked at Suleiman-bin-Daoud and saw the most wise King's eyes twinkle like stars on a frosty night, and he picked up his courage with both wings, and he put his head on one side and said, 'O King, live for ever! She *is* my wife; and you know what wives are like.'

Suleiman-bin-Daoud smiled in his beard and said, 'Yes, *I* know, little brother.'

'One must keep them in order somehow,' said the Butterfly, 'and she has been quarrelling with me all the morning. I said that to quiet her.'

And Suleiman-bin-Daoud said, 'May it quiet her. Go back to your wife, little brother, and let me hear what you say.'

Back flew the Butterfly to his wife, who was all of a twitter behind a leaf, and she said, 'He heard you! Suleiman-bin-Daoud himself heard you!'

'Heard me!' said the Butterfly. 'Of course he did. I meant him to hear me.'

'And what did he say? Oh, what did he say?'

'Well,' said the Butterfly, fanning himself most importantly, 'between you and me, my dear – of course I don't blame him, because his Palace must have cost a great deal and the oranges are just ripening, – he asked me not to stamp, and I promised I wouldn't.'

'Gracious!' said his wife, and sat quite quiet; but Suleiman-bin-Daoud lauged till the tears ran down his face at the impudence of the bad little Butterfly.

She held out her finger and whispered softly

Balkis the Most Beautiful stood up behind the tree among the red lilies and smiled to herself, for she had heard all this talk. She thought, 'If I am wise I can yet save my Lord from the persecutions of these quarrelsome Queens,' and she held out her finger and whispered softly to the Butterfly's Wife, 'Little woman, come here.'

Up flew the Butterfly's Wife, very frightened, and clung to Balkis's white hand.

Balkis bent her beautiful head down and whispered, 'Little woman, do you believe what your husband has just said?'

The Butterfly's Wife looked at Balkis, and saw the Most Beautiful

Queen's eyes shining like deep pools with starlight on them, and she picked up her courage with both wings and said, 'O Queen, be lovely for ever. *You* know what men-folk are like.'

And the Queen Balkis, the Wise Balkis of Sheba, put her hand to her lips to hide a smile, and said, 'Little sister, *I* know.'

'They get angry,' said the Butterfly's Wife, fanning herself quickly, 'over nothing at all, but we must humour them, O Queen. They never mean half they say. If it pleases my husband to believe that I believe he can make Suleiman-bin-Daoud's Palace disappear by stamping his foot, I'm sure *I* don't care. He'll forget all about it to-morrow.'

'Little sister,' said Balkis, 'you are quite right; but next time he begins to boast, take him at his word. Ask him to stamp, and see what will happen. *We* know what men-folk are like don't we? He'll be very much ashamed.'

Away flew the Butterfly's Wife to her husband, and in five minutes they were quarrelling worse than ever.

'Remember!' said the Butterfly. 'Remember what I can do if I stamp my foot.'

'I don't believe you one little bit,' said the Butterfly's Wife. 'I should very much like to see it done. Suppose you stamp now.'

'I promised Suleiman-bin-Daoud that I wouldn't,' said the Butterfly, 'and I don't want to break my promise.'

'It wouldn't matter if you did,' said his wife. 'You couldn't bend a blade of grass with your stamping. I dare you to do it,' she said. 'Stamp! Stamp! Stamp!'

Suleiman-bin-Daoud, sitting under the camphor-tree, heard every word of this, and he laughed as he had never laughed in his life before. He forgot all about his Queens; he forgot about the Animal that came out of

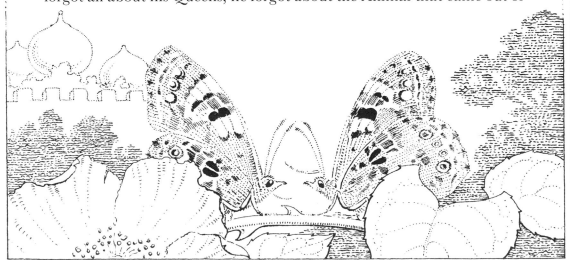

the sea; he forgot about showing off. He just laughed with joy, and Balkis, on the other side of the tree, smiled because her own true love was so joyful.

Presently the Butterfly, very hot and puffy, came whirling back under the shadow of the camphor-tree and said to Suleiman, 'She wants me to stamp! She wants to see what will happen, O Suleiman-bin-Daoud! You know I can't do it, and now she'll never believe a word I say. She'll laugh at me to the end of my days!'

'No, little brother,' said Suleiman-bin-Daoud, 'she will never laugh at you again,' and he turned the ring on his finger – just for the little Butterfly's sake, not for the sake of showing off, – and, lo and behold, four huge Djinns came out of the earth!

'Slaves,' said Suleiman-bin-Daoud, 'when this gentleman on my finger' (that was where the impudent Butterfly was sitting) 'stamps his left front forefoot you will make my Palace and these gardens disappear in a clap of thunder. When he stamps again you will bring them back carefully.'

'Now, little brother,' he said, 'go back to your wife and stamp all you've a mind to.'

Away flew the Butterfly to his wife, who was crying, 'I dare you to do it! I dare you to do it! Stamp! Stamp now! Stamp!' Balkis saw the four vast Djinns stoop down to the four corners of the gardens with the Palace in the middle, and she clapped her hands softly and said, 'At last Suleiman-bin-Daoud will do for the sake of a Butterfly what he ought to have done long ago for his own sake, and the quarrelsome Queens will be frightened!'

Then the Butterfly stamped. The Djinns jerked the Palace and the gardens a thousand miles into the air: there was a most awful thunder-clap, and everything grew inky black. The Butterfly's Wife fluttered about in the dark, crying, 'Oh, I'll be good! I'm so sorry I spoke! Only bring the gardens back, my dear darling husband, and I'll never contradict again.'

The Butterfly was nearly as frightened as his wife, and Suleiman-bin-Daoud laughed so much that it was several minutes before he found breath enough to whisper to the Butterfly, 'Stamp again, little brother. Give me back my Palace, most great magician.'

'Yes, give him back his Palace,' said the Butterfly's Wife, still flying about in the dark like a moth. 'Give him back his Palace, and don't let's have any more horrid magic.'

'Well, my dear,' said the Butterfly as bravely as he could, 'you see what your nagging has led to. Of course it doesn't make any difference to *me* – I'm used to this kind of thing – but as a favour to you and to Suleiman-bin-Daoud I don't mind putting things right.'

So he stamped once more, and that instant the Djinns let down the Palace and the gardens, without even a bump. The sun shone on the dark-

When suddenly the palace disappeared . . .

green orange-leaves; the fountains played among the pink Egyptian lilies; the birds went on singing; and the Butterfly's Wife lay on her side under the camphor-tree waggling her wings and panting, 'Oh, I'll be good! I'll be good!'

Suleiman-bin-Daoud could hardly speak for laughing. He leaned back all weak and hiccoughy, and shook his finger at the Butterfly and said, 'O great wizard, what is the sense of returning to me my Palace if at the same time you slay me with mirth?'

Then came a terrible noise, for all the nine hundred and ninety-nine Queens ran out of the Palace shrieking and shouting and calling for their babies. They hurried down the great marble steps below the fountain, one hundred abreast and the Most Wise Balkis went statelily forward to meet them and said, 'What is your trouble, O Queens?'

They stood on the marble steps one hundred abreast and shouted, '*What* is our trouble? We were living peacefully in our golden Palace, as is our custom, when upon a sudden the Palace disappeared, and we were left sitting in a thick and noisome darkness; and it thundered, and Djinns and Afrits moved about in the darkness! *That* is our trouble, O Head Queen, and we are most extremely troubled on account of that trouble, for it was a troublesome trouble, unlike any trouble we have known.'

Then Balkis the Most Beautiful Queen – Suleiman-bin-Daoud's Very Best Beloved – Queen that was of Sheba and Sabie and the Rivers of the Gold of the South – from the Desert of Zinn to the Towers of Zimbabwe – Balkis, almost as wise as the Most Wise Suleiman-bin-Daoud himself, said, 'It is nothing, O Queens! A Butterfly has made complaint against his wife because she quarrelled with him, and it has pleased our Lord Suleiman-bin-Daoud to teach her a lesson in low-speaking and humbleness, for that is counted a virtue among the wives of the butterflies.'

Then up and spoke an Egyptian Queen – the daughter of a Pharaoh – and she said, 'Our Palace cannot be plucked up by the roots like a leek for the sake of a little insect. No! Suleiman-bin-Daoud must be dead, and what we heard and saw was the earth thundering and darkening at the news.'

Then Balkis beckoned that bold Queen without looking at her, and said to her and to the others, 'Come and see.'

They came down the marble steps, one hundred abreast, and beneath his camphor-tree, still weak with laughing, they saw the Most Wise King Suleiman-bin-Daoud rocking back and forth with a Butterfly on either hand, and they heard him say, 'O wife of my brother in the air, remember after this to please your husband in all things, lest he be provoked to stamp his foot yet again; for he has said that he is used to this Magic, and he is most eminently a great magician – one who steals away the very Palace of Suleiman-bin-Daoud himself. Go in peace, little folk!' And he kissed them on the wings, and they flew away.

Then all the Queens except Balkis – the Most Beautiful and Splendid Balkis, who stood apart smiling – fell flat on their faces, for they said, 'If these things are done when a Butterfly is displeased with his wife, what shall be done to us who have vexed our King with our loud-speaking and open quarrelling through many days?'

Then they put their veils over their heads, and they put their hands over their mouths, and they tiptoed back to the Palace most mousy-quiet.

Then Balkis – the Most Beautiful and Excellent Balkis – went forward through the red lilies into the shade of the camphor-tree and laid her hand upon Suleiman-bin-Daoud's shoulder and said, 'O my Lord and Treasure of my Soul, rejoice, for we have taught the Queens of Egypt and Mesopotamia and Abyssinia and Persia and India and China with a great and a memorable teaching.'

And Suleiman-bin-Daoud, still looking after the Butterflies where they played in the sunlight, said, 'O my Lady and Jewel of my Felicity, when did this happen? For I have been jesting with a Butterfly ever since I came into the garden.' And he told Balkis what he had done.

Balkis – the Tender and Most Lovely Balkis said, 'O my Lord and Regent of my Existence, I hid behind the camphor-tree and saw it all. It was I who told the Butterfly's Wife to ask the Butterfly to stamp, because I hoped that for the sake of the jest my Lord would make some great Magic and that the Queens would see it and be frightened.' And she told him what the Queens had said and seen and thought.

Then Suleiman-bin-Daoud rose up from his seat under the camphor-tree, and stretched his arms and rejoiced and said, 'O my Lady and Sweetener of my Days, know that if I had made a Magic against my Queens for the sake of pride or anger, as I made that feast for all the animals, I should certainly have been put to shame. But by means of your wisdom I made the Magic for the sake of a jest and for the sake of a little Butterfly, and – behold – it has also delivered me from the vexations of my vexatious wives! Tell me, therefore, O my Lady and Heart of my Heart, how did you come to be so wise?'

And Balkis the Queen, beautiful and tall, looked up into Suleiman-bin-Daoud's eyes and put her head a little on one side, just like the Butterfly, and said, 'First, O my Lord, because I loved you; and secondly, O my Lord, because I know what women-folk are.'

Then they went up to the Palace and lived happily ever afterwards. But wasn't it clever of Balkis?

THE END